Lyrik's Song 2

A Novel Written By TesjamebraJ

Copyright © 2019, Self-Published

All rights reserved. No part of this book may be used or reproduced in any form or by any means electronic or mechanical, including photocopying, recording or by information storage and retrieval system, without the written permission from the author.

This novel is a work of fiction. Any resemblances to actual events, real people, living or dead, organizations, establishments or locales are products of the author's imagination. Other names, characters, places, and incidents are used fictitiously.

Chapter 1
Gia

"This one's in critical condition! We got to get him to the hospital!" The hatred in my heart intensified with every breathe Tyrek took. My sister took her life while this son of a bitch was still alive despite his wounds.

"He's my sister's husband. Can I come with you?"

"Yeah. Come on." The EMT in the ambulance helped me climb in next to him. Tyrek just laid there. Blood splattered. *My sister died for you.* I straightened my face as the EMTs worked to keep Tyrek alive. I wanted to stab his ass with one of these scalpels or needles in here. I had to think of the long game. I was not about to let him walk around while my sister was about to be 6 feet under. He lived today through the grace of God. The Lord works hard but I was about to work even harder to make sure this man did not take another breath.

Lyrik

The water in the shower had run cold. I stopped crying. Nothing else could come out. I ran out of tears to shed. I turned the water off and stepped out of the shower. I grabbed my towel and wrapped it around myself. I stood there in front of the sink and wiped the now foggy mirror with my hand. I couldn't believe all that happened tonight. I opened the medicine cabinet and got the ibuprofens and gauze. I wrapped my arm as tightly and delicately as possible. It may have been a graze, but I still wasn't about to let it just get infected or something. I could still hear the yelling and screaming in the front room. *Levi's still entertaining his guests.*

Normally, I would sleep in his room, but it just didn't feel right tonight. I got dressed in sweatpants and a t-shirt then walked to the bookshelf in my room filled with some of my favorite authors. Today was a toss-up between Reds Johnson and Robert Cost. I had just finished *Every Bullet Gotta Name 3,* so I decided to go with *Silver Platter Hoe 2*.

I settled into my bed, under my covers, and started reading. I got lost in the pages and didn't even hear Levi walk into my room.

"Why you didn't say you were home?" Levi sat down at the foot of my bed and I damn near jumped out of my skin.

"I didn't want to disturb you." My voice cracked from crying in the shower for what felt like hours. Levi was in good spirits until he saw my arm wrapped up in gauze and noticed the puffiness of my eyes.

"What happened?" Levi's voice was stern, protective.

"Shoot out at the club. It's not that serious."

"Not that serious? You could've died."

"But I didn't. I'm fine. I promise."

"And Claire?"

"She's fine."

"Who did the shooting?" *I shouldn't tell him… or should I?*

"I couldn't— "

"You're a terrible liar, Lyrik. Who did it?" I swallowed hard. I didn't want to deal with this right now.

"Tyrek and Tone." Levi hopped off my bed like he was ready to kill someone. I chased after him into his room. He was pacing back and forth. *Why is he pacing back and forth?*

Levi saw me standing in the doorway looking confused and instantly relaxed himself. *Was he contemplating hurting Tyrek?*

"I'm sorry. I'm just sick of you being hurt because of one man's stupid actions. Lyrik, I want you safe."

"You don't have to worry about any of that anymore. Tyrek and Tone didn't make it."

"Wait what?"

"They're dead." Levi looked at me in disbelief. He grabbed the remote from the nightstand to turn on the TV to see if the shooting made it to the 11 o'clock news.

We've just arrived at the scene of a shooting at Club Exclusive. So far, the police have confirmed that two civilians have died from gunshot wounds while another civilian is in critical condition. LaBrielle Allen and Antonio "Tone" Ashford have been pronounced dead at the scene of the crime. Tyrek Williams is said to be in critical condition and undergoing surgery in order to try to retrieve the bullet that is said to be dangerously close to his spine. We'll keep you updated as the story develops.

Levi and I both looked on in shock as the news reporter continued to the next segment.

"But I saw him get shot…"

"They said that he's in critical condition. The bullet hit a vital organ or something. They said it was close to his spine. It probably went through one of his lungs."

"I can't believe that he's alive. Of all the people that died tonight, he was the one that lived. Unbelievable."

"I'm just glad that you aren't hurt." Levi cradled me in his arms and held me. I never felt so safe or secure as I did when he headed me. Levi was a dream come true. He was something out of the movies.

"I'm glad that I'm safe too." I was confused on how to feel about Tyrek being alive but in critical condition. Tone was dead and LaBrielle was dead. This didn't seem like reality.

Claire

Even with all the bullshit that Tone put me through, I should've been the bigger person. I shouldn't have turned my back on him. Not completely. He and Tyrek were always so close. It just didn't make sense for them to be shooting at each other over a few words.

Tone's past must've caught up with him in a big way. Karma was a bitch and she never miss. When I got home, Miguel had a bath ran and my favorite meal cooked. *What did I do to deserve this man?*

I sat in Miguel's lap as he fed me. I almost forgot all about Tone. The constant pampering was amazing. Almost too good to be true.

"I love you, Claire." Miguel had never outright told me that he loved me, but his actions spoke volumes.

"I love you too."

Miguel led me to the bathroom of his apartment and began to wash away all my sorrows. Of all the women that were constantly chasing him, he decided to choose me. He chose me in a crowd of many. He bathed away all my troubles, all my doubt, all my guilt. Miguel made me feel worthy of his love and attention. Like I was enough. I never felt that way with Tone. *Why am I still thinking of Tone?*

Chapter 2
Levi

Tyrek being in critical condition threw me for a loop. The fact that Lyrik was even in that kind of danger – Lyrik could've been the one in a coffin instead of Tone. Nothing else mattered to me. Lyrik's safety was all I cared about. Tyrek was a thorn in my side, and he was barely even alive. He was fighting for his life and all I wanted to do was beat his ass for starting a damn shootout.

Times like this I wanted to tell Lyrik the truth about me – about what I've been doing these past few weeks. I had gone through so much trying to conceal everything to the point of no return. Lyrik would lose all hope if she knew the truth. I was the one that saved her from a bad place. I wouldn't be responsible for sending her over the edge. I couldn't do that to her. I would tell her at the right time but now just wasn't the right time.

Gia

I stayed at the hospital for three hours until I was told that I would have to go to the police station for questioning. I still had on the same blood-stained outfit as before. They told me to go home and get cleaned up but how could I go back to that house without Brielle?

I lost Brielle and Tyrek got to keep his life? Bullshit. He played me and other girls like a fucking fiddle to get what he wanted. Lyrik was the only one smart enough to not fall for the shit that constantly rolled off his tongue. Tyrek was a smooth operator and a fighter, but this fight was one that I refused to let him win.

I couldn't go back to that apartment. I bought some clothes and rented a motel room with the small amount that I did have. *Maybe things will be better tomorrow.*

The hot water poured down on me and it seemed to melt away my sins. If only for a moment…I felt normal. For a moment, I felt that everything was going to be okay…until I heard a knock at the door.

I got out the shower and put on my clothes as quickly as possible. I was not about to be caught slipping. Especially not now. Everybody knew about Tyrek. I wasn't safe anymore. I had to find my own way now. I was strapped for weapons, but the motel did have a complimentary iron in each room. *That's gonna have to do for now.*

"Who is it?" No answer. "I said 'who is it'?" No answer. I started to lower my defenses but the banging on the door got louder, more desperate. Iron in hand, I opened the door. A tall dark-skinned man ran inside and locked the door behind him. The sirens that were once indistinct became louder then indistinct again as they drove by the motel.

"Took you long enough to open the door…"

"Sorry but I don't usually open the door when a muthafucka banging at it. Especially not when the cops are after said person." He laughed at my response. Or maybe he laughed at the fact that I had an iron in my hand and I wasn't about to loosen my grip.

"Look, I'm Duke." He reached out his hand for a handshake. The only thing I could do was timidly look at him and his outstretched hand. "I won't bite." I rolled my eyes and shook his hand.

"Gia. Now, can you get out of my room?"

"Why a pretty girl like you in this dump anyway?"

"None of your business."

"You a prostitute huh?"

"What?! Nigga, no!"

"What is it then?"

"Who the fuck are you to be questioning me about shit? Are you gonna take care of me or something?"

"Damn. I can't be concern 'bout 'chu?" Duke's playful attitude was getting on my nerves and he needed to leave. But at the same time, I wouldn't mind a little companionship after the night I had. I needed a friend. Someone to talk to.

"Look, my night was pretty fucked up. I'm not in the mood." Duke could clearly see the frustration on my face. His demeanor became more serious.

"Well, look here, how 'bout I break you off a couple bills and I'll just come back later and check up on you?" Duke handed me a money roll of what looked like a couple thousand dollars.

"I can't accept this."

"Think of it as payment for saving my ass. I'll see you 'round the way, Angel."

"My name is Gia!"

"I know. I called you 'Angel' because you got the face of one. Don't trip, Lil Bit." Duke proceeded to exit out the door. I was still in shock at the fact that this stranger gave me a couple stacks just because. No man ever gave me anything just because. Before my mama died and LaBrielle got custody of me, my own daddy was nothing more than a disappointment.

He got my mama pregnant then dipped. The first time I met him was at a clinic to get tested cause he was convinced that I wasn't his. When the results proved that I was his disappeared completely, got married, had kids with his new wife and sent some money here and there. I'd only met my half siblings maybe once or twice. LaBrielle didn't have to worry about any of that. Her dad was married to mom at one point. His death broke our mother. I don't think she ever healed from the loss.

The thought of someone doing anything nice for me, just for the sake of being nice, was a bullshit notion. A fantasy. There was no such thing as free. There was always a price to pay.

Claire

I drove to Levi and Lyrik's new house in an attempt to calm my nerves. Lyrik said that she had troubles sleeping and that she had something to tell me. With everything that happened, I couldn't imagine what could be worse than the deaths that occurred the other night.

"Hey." Lyrik greeted me. She looked worn out. I guess what happened really took a toll on her. The bandage on her arm was the proof. Lyrik got caught in the crossfire. I know that wasn't easy to explain to Levi.

"Hey."

Lyrik and Levi's love nest looked amazing. It definitely had enough space. The house looked like it was decorated by Lyrik with a few inputs from Levi. It wasn't extra girly, but it didn't look like a bachelor pad either. I was glad that through it all, Lyrik had somehow found her happily ever after.

Lyrik led me to the couch in the den where we sat and discussed what happened the night of the shooting. What shocked me was when Lyrik told me about Tyrek. Tyrek wasn't dead. Instead, he was now in ICU. In all honesty, I felt even worse after hearing that. Tyrek caused a ripple in our pond when he came back home. Nothing was the same.

Our entire circle imploded and there was nothing any of us could do to stop it. We all played our hand – we just didn't know how deadly it would be.

Chapter 3
Gia

I could not believe that even with my statement to the police, Tyrek wasn't going to be charged for Tone's death due to it being "self-defense". Everything about the case was pure bullshit. The cops here acted like they didn't care about the black bodies that hit the pavement. I wasn't shocked in the least bit, but I hoped that something would be different.

LaBrielle's funeral was being planned by me while Claire helped Tone's grandmother with his arrangements. Claire offered to help me bury LaBrielle, but it didn't feel right knowing all the shit that LaBrielle and I drug her through. We both had ties with Tone and it just didn't sit well with me. When I pulled up to the funeral home, I just felt sick to my stomach. We had our differences but LaBrielle was my sister. I did this to my sister.

"Hi. My name is Gia…"

"You're the one burying your sister. We'll be right with you. I'm so sorry for your loss." The receptionist seemed genuine. You could tell who the veterans were and who were the rookies when it came to death. The ones who have worked in a mortuary for years seemed dead themselves. The idea of death was nothing more than a natural end. We all had to die at some time.

"Are you 'Ms. Allen'?" A voice behind me boomed. Turned around to see Duke standing behind a man that was clearly the owner of the funeral home.

"Yes. I am. I'm here to make arrangements for my sister, LaBrielle."

"Yes. I heard about it on the news. I'm sorry you have to go through this all alone. Y'all didn't have any family?" *He's been doing this a while.*

"No. It was just the two of us."

"Well, my son is going to help you pick out caskets and her flowers. I'm sorry that I can't be with you, but I have an emergency to attend to. Duke, make sure you take care of her in her time of need." With that, he scurried off and Duke led me to a room full of the prettiest caskets that I had ever seen.

"So, these are –"

"So, you just gonna act like you don't know me?" I crossed my arms and stared Duke up and down. He looked completely different from the last time that I saw him. His black t-shirt, jeans and black Chuck Taylor's were now converted into a black Armani suit with matching black loafers. The suit looked like it was tailored to fit his frame.

"Look, I'm just trying to be professional. Plus, you need to look at caskets, right?"

"I can't afford these."

"What about the money that I gave you?"

"That money isn't going to cover the whole funeral. Plus, I had to get a car and hire movers to get everything out of the apartment that I shared with my sister."

"Let me guess… You need a job too? Or are you still hookin'?"

"I'm not a prostitute. I've never had a job. I was always taken care of. So, I'm just tryna figure some things out. I can't stay at that sleazy ass motel." Duke looked at me with sympathetic eyes. He took a deep breath and let out a sigh before he answered.

"Stay with me."

"Excuse me?"

"You need somewhere to stay. And before your loud mouth ass say anything, I'm hardly ever home anyway."

"Nah, why you being so nice to me?"

"I can't be nice?"

"Not without a price. Everybody wants something in return. What do you want?"

"Let me take you out?"

"Like on a date?"

"Yeah."

"No." I turned to walk out the door, but he grabbed my wrist.

"Why not?"

"Why would I?" I snatched my wrist back and walked out the door. I was parked close to the entrance, so I got in my 2016 Toyota Corolla and just sat there to process what just happened. Nobody had ever taken me on a date before. I've never even been asked. All I knew about relationships, I learned from watching LaBrielle and I knew that that was not the example that I should be following. The thoughts in my mind were scrambled and I didn't even realize that Duke followed me outside. When Duke knocked on the driver's side window, I nearly jumped out of my skin. I only rolled down the window slightly, just enough for him to be able to hear me.

"Look, I'm sorry if I made you uncomfortable, but there are decent people in the world."

"Decent?"

"Yeah."

"Why were you running from the cops?"

"What?"

"'What?' When we first met, you were running from the cops. Why?"

"I was taking care of some business."

"You're a drug dealer."

"No. I don't deal anything."

"So, what then? You smuggle shit?"

"You a cop or something? Why you wanna know my life story but won't let me take you out to eat?" I couldn't do anything but try to hold back the smile that was coming to the surface as I shook my head in disbelief. "There's a smile. Let me take you out and I'll let you know a few things about me."

"Fine. But I get to pick the restaurant."

"Okay. Just say when." Duke handed me his phone and I gave him my number. A distraction was necessary. I just hoped that he didn't want more.

After leaving the mortuary, I instantly went to the hospital. Tyrek was still in critical condition and he was unresponsive. I had to tell everybody I was his sister in order to even get in his room. The dimly lit room looked so peaceful. Tyrek didn't deserve peace. LaBrielle frequently worked at the hospital and would steal needles for the local drug addicts as her way of giving back. I guess she figured that you can't help someone quit if they weren't ready. Today her stealing needles came in handy. I reached into my small purse and prepared the empty needle then stuck it in Tyrek's IV. It's funny how the air could cause more issues that an allergic reaction to whatever medicine they could prescribe. Within seconds, Tyrek was having convulsions. I wiped my fingerprints off the needle then threw it in the biohazard container in the corner. The heart monitor went steady and the nurses and doctors rushed in. I pretended to have a breakdown. I pretended to not want to leave his side. I even fought off doctors to maintain my innocence. Two security guards had to drag me out the room. The tears that fell down my face sealed the deal. They forced me into the waiting room while they attempted to save his life, but it was too late. Tyrek was gone and I felt so much better. Although LaBrielle was a casualty, it felt good to not have to worry about Tyrek ever again.

Lyrik

Everything seemed like it was going back to normal. My wound was almost completely healed, and Levi was progressing as a lawyer. He may have been a rookie, but his numbers resembled that of a veteran. I was proud of Levi. Every day he would come home from work and tell me about his day, and he would ask about mine. It was like he was the superhero that came and took me away from everything.

Levi was the light in my life that made everything else brighter too. We even went on double – and sometimes triple – dates with Jamal and Sahara or Claire and Miguel. My relationship with Sahara improved tremendously and we were even in therapy to find the root of our problems with each other.

Everything seemed to be going well. After moving in with Levi, I used the money I saved up from Tyrek over the years to buy me a car. Nothing too fancy but it got me from point A to point B and back again. Things were looking up.

"It seems to me like you were jealous of Lyrik, Sahara. Why is that?" Dr. Jones asked. This was just one of many therapy sessions. Sahara didn't want to admit her truths. She wanted to move forward and never speak on it again, but I wasn't like that. I needed to heal. I needed to know the source of Sahara's hatred for me.

"Growing up, I would constantly hear about how gorgeous Lyrik was. I was the dark skinned one and she was the pretty light skinned one. I didn't get the attention she got."

"So that made you resentful?"

"Yes. I hated Lyrik. Every boyfriend I had liked her and complimented her. Lyrik was a virgin and was getting all this attention. And she didn't even want the attention. Meanwhile, I had to lose my virginity at an early age just to get the same amount of attention. I started getting called 'easy'. I just couldn't understand why. What was it about me that just couldn't compare?" Sahara's voice began to break as the tears began to fall. This was the first time I had ever heard Sahara cry. Let alone explain her disdain for me.

"Lyrik, how do you feel after hearing your sister's confession?"

"I don't know how to feel. I love my sister. I always have. I just feel like our mother was the driving force behind the hate that Sahara had for me. I was told how much I looked like my father growing up and that pissed my mother off. The anger and rage that she would –" I couldn't even continue without crying. I hadn't thought about my mother and her abuse in a while. It was clear that me and my sister were both traumatized by her actions.

"What I see is that Lyrik believes that your mother contributed to your belief that Lyrik was better. She implanted that hatred in you and made you help her lash out on Lyrik because Lyrik resemble your father. Do you believe that Sahara?"

"I never thought about it before now. Looking back on it, I do. She would constantly tell me that Lyrik walked around like she was better than both of us. It pissed me off. 'How can she even begin to think that she was better than us?' My mother turned me into a monster. A colorist. I hated my sister, I hated her light skin. I was jealous of her light skin."

"But I looked up to you." I interjected. The pain in my voice caused Sahara to shutter.

"And I looked up to her."

Chapter 4
Levi

Every Friday when Lyrik went to her therapy sessions with Sahara, I was at the local rehab facility. I visited frequently but this time was different. This time it was time to bring her home. Like would probably hate me but she would have to forgive me eventually. *Hopefully.*

***

"Lyrik always did take a liking to you. I'm surprised that y'all are just now a 'thing'. What has she been up to?"

"Undoing all the damage that you caused. Her and Sahara are at a therapist office now."

"I was a horrible mother to both of them. I just hope and pray that they can forgive me."

"It might take more than an apology but getting clean was the first step forward."

If there was ever a Worst Parent Ever award, Nailah Pauline Moore would win every year. Nailah abused Lyrik frequently. I helped cover the bruises, the cuts, the scraps. Nailah was lucky that she was a woman; otherwise, I would have beat her ass for all that she did to Lyrik. Nailah caused a shit ton of grief that both Lyrik and Sahara had to heal from. Nailah's turn to heal. I couldn't have Nailah live with me and Lyrik; so, I set her up at a nearby hotel. I had to ease Lyrik into the possibility of her mother being in her life. It was bad enough that I found Nailah in at the police station a few weeks ago while I was visiting a client. Nailah was so skinny that her ribs were visible through her shirt. She looked sickly and malnourished. When she saw me, she knew who I was immediately. She begged me for help, and I couldn't turn her away. Lyrik meant everything to me and if she could repair her relationship with Sahara then Nailah could be forgiven for her sins as well. Lyrik needed family.

When we arrived at the hotel, I checked Nailah in and gave her my number in case of emergency. I didn't want her to call frequently and have Lyrik suspicious of me. I wanted Nailah to be a part of Lyrik's life. She was Lyrik's mother.

"If you can't get in touch with me, just shoot me a text. This phone only has my number in it. Don't pawn it and don't backtrack into the person you were before. I went out of my way to get you sober and you will stay sober. Do you understand me?" Lyrik's mother was Sahara's twin. Dark skinned with the smoothest skin. If you didn't know her personally, you wouldn't have thought she was a recovering alcoholic and drug addict. She had gained some of her weight back and she was a naturally beautiful woman. Lyrik needed more family and a better support system in her life. I just hoped that Lyrik could forgive me one day.

Gia

I wasn't used to this. A fancy night out with an attentive man? Never. A quick fuck session with an immature little boy? Definitely. I had never been on a date and the thought of being on one made me sick but in a good way. Duke really went all out. He took me out the state just for a date. We ended up in Atlanta and everything just continued to get better. He was the ultimate gentleman. Duke opened doors, pulled out chairs; he even brought me flowers. I had never experienced anything like this.

I felt special. I felt vulnerable. I liked the feeling but at the same time I didn't. I didn't like feeling fuzzy and shit. Being vulnerable was a liability in the streets. Being vulnerable was LaBrielle and Tyrek's undoing.

"You seem distracted." I looked up from the restaurant's menu. Duke was staring me dead into my eyes. His dark brown eyes were piercing my soul.

"I'm fine. My sister's funeral is in a couple days. I just – I can't believe that she's gone." I tried to hold back my tears as much as possible. I wasn't weak. I would never show anyone the sensitive side of me. I hated to cry in front of people. Whether I was hurt or not, no one would every know.

"I can understand that. My cousin going under soon. He was like my brother. But he was into that street life shit and I wasn't. I just came back into town when I heard about what happened. He was supposed to show me a good time. It had been a long time since I had been here. I get where you coming from." The look in Duke's eyes let me know that he was hurting. He felt the same pain that I felt when it came to losing a loved one. Duke could relate to me and it made our night that much more special. That loss that we both had to endure is what was gonna make us stronger.

"I'm sorry about your cousin."

"I'm sorry about your sister."

"May the both rest in peace."

"And may their killers rest in pieces." *If only you knew.*

Duke

Gia was the most beautiful woman I had ever seen. I wasn't the type to chase after nobody, but I could tell that she was worth it. The way she refused my help at every turn even though she never had to lift a finger showed me that she was more that just some spoiled brat. When necessary, she come go out and chase the bag herself. That's the time of woman I needed. I had to have her. I wasn't about to let her slip through my fingers.

"You and your sister were close, huh?" *Why would you ask that and she still grieving?*

"Yeah. After our mom died, she became somewhat of a mom." Her face was emotionless. She was hard to read, and I could tell that that was intentional.

"You always bottle up your feelings?" She put down her menu and looked at me with her arms crossed.

"Why you so worried?" *Defensive as hell.*

"I can't ask a question?"

"You can't answer mine?"

"Maybe I like you. Ever think about that?"

"You like me until I give you some ass." She muttered under her breath. She picked back up her menu and continued to browse.

"I would tear that ass up, make you a wife, and have you pregnant with my baby after just a few dates. You will fall so deeply in love with me that nothing I ask of you will be too much. Don't underestimate my feelings for you. Ever." Gia instantly sat up in her seat and I could tell that I had her attention. I knew that nobody had ever been that straightforward and blunt before. I wasn't about games and I wasn't about to let anything, or anyone get in my way.

"Are the two of you ready to order?" I hadn't even noticed that the waitress was waiting to take our orders. I decided to be risky and do something that I'm sure Gia had never experienced.

"I'll have the chicken penne with crostini and the lady will have the broccoli pesto." Gia looked at me like I was crazy, but she didn't object.

"Very good. And would you like another glass of Domaine Ramonet Montrachet Grand Cru?"

"Just bring the whole bottle. Thank you."

"I'll be right back."

"You have some major balls to order for me." Gia spat out after the waitress told our menus and left.

"I'm just observant. You've never been to a restaurant this fancy; so, you were looking for the cheapest item on the menu which is why you were so fidgety."

Gia

He noticed that?

"I just didn't wanna be *that* girl." Duke chuckled softly. *That smile.*

"What kinda girl is that?"

"The type that's a gold diggin' cum dumpster."

"Well damn."

"Just sayin'." I took another sip of wine and started to relax a little. I knew Duke had influence when he ordered wine and they didn't even bother to card me.

"You could never be that girl. You're too smart and too gorgeous." I couldn't help but roll my eyes. *This is one suave muthafucka...*

"Tell me about yourself. You seem to know so much about me. What about you? How was life growing up?" Duke smiled and shrugged.

"What do you wanna know?"

"Everything."

Duke

Just like that I was inclined to discuss my childhood with this magnificent woman. She wanted to know everything, but she wasn't ready for the illegal parts. I wasn't ready to tell her how me and my cousin would run the streets talkin' mad shit. She wasn't ready to be my trap queen. Not yet. I gave her a simplistic answer.

"Not much to tell. I was a runt. Worked my way up. I had to hustle for everything I ever had or will get."

"Sounds like me."

"I thought you said you never had to lift a finger?"

"Don't underestimate me. I meant legally."

"Fair enough." *Maybe she is ready…*

My mother was addicted to drugs, so I spent most of my time at my grandmother's house. My cousin taught me the facts of the game each time he came to visit until I was real to start hustling. Shit went left though. I was forced to make a way out of no way and from there on, I elevated through the ranks. I was no longer the average drug dealer, I was the distributor. I was a protégé of Emilio Sosa. He had territory all over the world. Cuba, Colombia, Mexico... None of the cartels were able to do what he had done. He built an empire and he saw the same hunger in me. Emilio sold his drugs through the cartels and made billions of dollars. No one even knew his name. He was a ghost. Having any type of meeting with him was an honor, a privilege that wasn't afforded to many. He treated me like his son; so, I always received his presence whenever I went out the country or out the state to see him.

"What kinda name is 'Duke' anyway?" She joked before putting the wine glass up to her lips. I couldn't help but smile. Everything about her put me in a good mood.

"Funny. It's a nickname. My father's name is Dukesford."

"Wait..."

"Yes, I know. It's bad. But my grandparents named him after my grandfather; so, it is what it is. My real name is Maliek but growing up people would always say how I looked like my father. 'Lil Duke' this and 'Lil Duke' that."

"Uh-huh. So, from there came the name 'Duke'?"

"Yeah."

"I like Maliek though. It's cute." The waitress came out right on time with a waiter in tow with our food.

"Here we go." She sat the bottle of Domaine Ramonet Montrachet Grand Cru on ice next to me.

"Chicken penne with crostino. Broccoli pesto. Will that be all for you?" The waiter asked.

"Yes. Thank you." Gia assured. I had never had a woman make me blush, but I was blushing and smiling hard as hell at Gia. They gracefully departed and I watched Gia silently pray over her food before partaking.

A woman that prays. And is unapologetic about it. A rarity. The look on Gia's face let me know that she loved the food that I picked out for her.

"It's good ain't it?" I teased. I couldn't help but to tease Gia. She went from savoring her food to eating fast as hell. Like she hadn't eaten this good in weeks. *She probably hadn't.*

"Um... I'm sorry." Gia covered her full mouth to speak then placed her fork beside her plate. She straightened her posture and resumed her almost regal façade. When she continued to eat, she looked almost childlike. As if I had scolded her. As if I had told her to mind her manners.

"I didn't mean to make you uncomfortable." Gia placed her fork beside her plate once more and looked at me dejectedly.

"I — I should go." Gia got up quickly and I followed.

"Gia, we're in a whole other state."

"We need to leave now!"

"Okay okay. I'll go pay and get everything squared away. Okay?"

"Yeah."

"Wait here."

"Okay!" Gia's voice started breaking, almost like she was holding back tears. I paid for our meal and took our food to go. I wasn't sure what cause the change in Gia, but I hoped that when she was ready that she would tell me.

Chapter 5
Claire

Things between Miguel and I have been rocky to say the least since the shooting. It was like everywhere I went, Tone was there. Judging me. *Did I move on too quickly? Should I have given him a chance?* It felt like this was all my fault even though I knew that it wasn't. Between going to Tone's grandmother's house to make preparations and balancing my relationship with Miguel and school... My life was becoming a never-ending shit fest.

"I think red roses would be best. He hated anything tacky and he swore that he was royalty. I can't believe that Tyrek could do something so heinous. Him and Antonio were brothers." Grandma Patty was down lower than I had ever seen her. She raised

Tone when his parents abandoned him. His fate was the same as his father's and it pained her to deal with it.

"Tone did always say that Tyrek was like a brother to him." I let out a soft chuckle with reminiscing on the past.

"Not like brothers. They were brothers." I snapped my neck in Grandma Patty's direction, unblinking.

"Say what?"

"They shared a mother. My oldest. Antonio was the oldest but at the time of his birth his mother convinced herself that she wasn't ready for a child. She wanted to be an actress. I raised him myself while she ran off to be with Tyrek's father. Antonio's father died in prison before he could even meet him. Tyrek had a mother. As drugged out as she became, the life she offered him was much better than anything she ever offered Antonio." The confession made a single tear fall down my eye. *All this time…*

"I can't believe it."

"He went looking for her you know. Antonio found her drugged up somewhere. She told him about his brother. How he was so much better. When Antonio met Tyrek, his entire life went downhill. He got into the streets heavy, Tyrek followed suit. The difference was that Antonio was not built for that life. I didn't raise him that way. Tyrek, however, was. Antonio hated his mother for abandoning him, but he was the one that grew up in a loving home. Tyrek grew up in a broken home. Issa knew she couldn't take care of Antonio, so she did what was best. She couldn't take care of Tyrek either, but she wouldn't give him to me and his grandfather. I begged her for Tyrek. I begged and pleaded for that boy. But no… Tyrek never even knew the true nature of his relationship with Antonio. Antonio never told him. Antonio just hated him from a distance. I thought the animosity left as they got older but once Antonio got Tyrek arrested, I knew then that that was only the beginning. I knew." Grandma Patty began to sob uncontrollably, and I held her close. She lost her only child, her husband, and both of her grandchildren in a period of five years. The strength that she has had to endure was staggering and made what I was going through seem meager.

***

I left Grandma Patty's house with a new outlook on life. I had been ignoring Miguel and treating him like shit because I was grieving a man that treated me like shit when he was alive.

I rushed home to be with Miguel. I wasn't about to be away from him for another minute. I had been ignoring Miguel and doing him dirty for days. I was treating him unfairly due to me mourning; he did not deserve any of the hate that he received. I had to apologize for my actions.

When I got to the apartment complex, I rushed to my floor so that I could get to my man. Miguel was supposed to be off today and tomorrow, so I decided to make the most out of it.

"Sweetie, I love you too. No. No. I'll have to see, okay? I love you. Okay. Bye." Those words were the most painful to hear. When Miguel noticed me in the living room, his face went pale.

I tried to run back out of the door with tears in my eyes. Miguel was hot on my trail. He grabbed my arm before I even made it to the elevator.

"Get off of me! Get off you son of a bitch!" I cried. I tried to shake Miguel off of me, but he just fought harder to keep me close.

"I know what you think you heard but Claire, I can explain. It's not what you think."

"You were just telling someone else that you love them. And I know you don't talk to your mother like that. You and your mother aren't even getting along right now because you're with a 'negrita' or whatever the hell she called me."

"Claire, calm down. Come back to the apartment and I promise, I will explain everything. Please." My mind was telling me *'Girl, fuck him! This is Tone and those ol' phony ass lies all over again...'* My heart on the other hand was telling me that I should trust him. Miguel had not shown any signs of infidelity since the day that I meet him. He was nothing but caring. I never experienced anything quite like it before. I didn't even realize that I was walking back to the apartment with my hand in his. *I can't believe that I let this man punk me.* I had gone through hell with Tone and I refused to repeat that pattern with Miguel. We walked into the apartment and he sat me down on the couch. He sat opposite of me and held my hands in his. *It's something serious…*

"Claire, I love you." *It's really serious.* "I would never do anything to harm you."

"Then explain what I heard. You can't say that you love me without giving me the explanation that I deserve." I went through a lot with Tone. *Why is he always on my mind?*

"You're right. Claire, I have two daughters. I was on the phone with one of them."

"Wait, you have kids?! Where the fuck were you gonna tell me that?!" I was not expecting that.

"I co-parent with their mother but she's been keeping them from me lately."

"Why?"

"Because of you. Because I have a new woman in my life."

"You expect me to believe that? That you aren't sneaking around and fuckin' her when you aren't fuckin' me?"

"Are you that hurt to where you can't tell when someone truly cares about you?! I love you! I did not expect for you to find out this way, but it happened! I will not sit here and allow you to question my love for you when I'm trying to be the man for you. The man that you need, that you crave. You do you shut me out?" I didn't even have an answer. Miguel just ripped me to shreds and all my ass could think to do was cry. He instantly calmed down and wrapped me in his arms. I was undeserving of his mercy, of his love.

"What are their names?"

"Mariana and Marisol. They're twins."

"If we are going to be together then you have to find a way to take care of them. Get custody if you can. But you are not going to be an absentee father because your baby mama is still in love with you."

Lyrik

I knew just by the way that Levi was acting that he was planning something, but today wasn't the day. Claire was going to need my help getting through the day. Today was the day that Tone and LaBrielle were being laid to rest.

Levi claimed he was uncomfortable with going to Tone's funeral, but he would go for me. I loved that about Levi. He was always so selfless. Levi was uncomfortable but because I needed him, he was there.

***

When got to the church early to help Claire with the floral arrangements and to help pass out programs, but what I didn't expect was for Gia to be at the funeral.

"Lyrik, I'm glad that you're here. This is Gia, LaBrielle's sister. She's paying her respects before she has to be across town at Revelation for LaBrielle's funeral." Claire explained. Gia and LaBrielle definitely favored each other so it wasn't hard to tell that it was her. Gia shook hands with Levi first then me.

"I've actual been meaning to meet with you. There's some things that we have to discuss." *What the fuck do we have to discuss?* I was confused by the statement, but I followed Gia outside the church anyway.

"What is it that we need to talk about?"

"I know that you and my sister did not get along, but it wasn't because y'all truly disliked each other. Tyrek was the cause of your hatred towards each other. I know that it may be much to ask but I hope that you make time to come to her burial site for a final goodbye. If you don't, I understand completely. If you decide to, I'll be waiting." Gia walked off and got in the car with some guy. They drove off and I was left standing in front of the church with conflicted feelings. What Gia said about LaBrielle was true. I wasn't one to fight the other woman but when she decided to talk shit and try to fight me, I had to prove myself. I wasn't about to let her get away with anything. Looking back on it, I should've been the bigger woman. *Fuck!*

I walked back inside the church and immediately looked for Claire. When I saw her talking to Miguel, I stopped dead in my tracks. The conversation was definitely heated but I wasn't sure if I should stay or go. I had never seen Claire so upset before.

"You can leave! I didn't ask you to be here!"

"You didn't really give me a choice either. Claire, I love you but lately –"

"What? What's wrong now?! You have been annoying as hell."

"Claire!" I couldn't stay silent. Claire had crossed a boundary that should have never been crossed. I dragged her from in front of Miguel to the women's restroom. Claire was really on one. I wasn't sure what her deal was, but I knew it was deeper than what she let on. "What's wrong with you? You were just in love a few days ago and now you're acting like you hate Miguel's presence."

"It's not like that. You don't know anything about our relationship."

"Oh please! What could have possibly happened that made you hate him like this?"

"He has twin daughters and he didn't tell me. I live with him and had no clue that he had children. Not a picture or anything."

"Maybe because he was scared that you were going to act like this. You're not doing anything but confirming his initial fears." Claire broke down crying and her mascara instantly started running. I held her and tried to clean her face, but the tears kept flowing. "Claire, talk to me. What's wrong?" Claire calmed enough to catch her breath.

"I-I-I" Claire began to stutter but she took a deep breath and calmly cleared her mind.

"I'm pregnant, Lyrik. If he's not in the life of the kid's that he already has, then why would he be there for my kid?"

"Just because he's not in their life doesn't mean that he doesn't want to be. Bitter baby mamas do and say some evil shit. My mother kept my father away from me and Sahara for so long until I think he just gave up. Claire, you have to tell him the truth instead of being angry towards him."

"Everybody's waiting." Grandma Patty came in the restroom to inform us. She looked at Claire's face and instantly became the nurturing woman we all know and love. "What's wrong?" Claire looked at her like a lost puppy and continued to sob some more.

"I'm pregnant."

"Well, that's a blessing. Why are you crying?"

"Because I'm still in love with Tone and the baby might not be Miguel's."

Claire's confession hit me like a ton of bricks. Claire was usually calculated in everything that she did. Her admitting that the child growing in her stomach may not belong to Miguel was beyond shocking. *If Miguel isn't the father, then who is?*

Levi

"Everything okay with Claire?" Lyrik looked discombobulated as hell.

"Uh… Yeah. Everything's fine."

"Okay. Good. Miguel seems a lil on edge but he's good." My phone started ringing extra loud and I already knew who it was. With the service about to start, I wasn't surprised that Nailah decided to call out of the blue.

"Who's that?"

"Work. Let me see what they want real quick and I'll be right back."

"Okay." I couldn't walk to the back and answer quick enough.

"What do you want?"

I want to see my daughter. I thought that you said I would be able to see her today. Why have I not seen Lyrik or Sahara?

"You just got clean. We can set up a meeting, but you are not going to force this on her. Not after everything that you put her through."

Fine. But I will not be ignored.

"Yeah." Nailah was really blowing my high. She knew that Lyrik and Sahara were in therapy and trying to get over her abuse. I said that I would see if they would be willing to meet up with her and it just went left from there. I walked back in toward the front of the church when I bumped into Jazmine coming out of the women's restroom. *Fuck!*

"Well, lookie here. Levi Hendrix. How have you been?" Jazmine seemed cool but I knew she had an ulterior motive.

"I'm fine. I hope that you are also well."

"I'm great considering…"

"I should go find my seat." My legs couldn't carry me quick enough to get away from Jazmine.

"That suit looks great on you."

"Thank you."

***

The pastor began to preach about life and death, and I couldn't help but to notice that Jazmine was staring at me from a distance. I felt her staring and she was unphased when I stared back. Lyrik even caught Jazmine staring. I knew then that this was not about to end well. Jazmine was staring way too hard for comfort and Lyrik was getting more and more pissed off by the second. I just hope that the Lord grant me the power to be able to get through this funeral in one piece.

Gia

My sister looked so beautiful in her casket. She was draped in white lace and jewels galore. LaBrielle was more than just my sister, she was my mother from an early age. I told her for granted but I wasn't about to let her have a shitty homegoing. My sister was about to have the best of the best. The irony about the entire situation is that Duke paid for everything. I hadn't talked to him since our awkward date. He clearly kept tabs on me though because he bought everything that I said I wanted for my sister. Duke was truly a different breed.

Duke sent me a text to send his condolences and to let me know that he wouldn't be in attendance. He told me to call him after the funeral so that we could talk, and I knew instantly that he wanted to converse about our date. I panicked and caused a scene. I never let my guard down around any man and I hadn't intended to do so with Duke. It made things complicated.

Duke buying everything for the funeral made me feel so type of way. My sister was going to be laid to rest as a queen. She was going to be buried how I wanted her to be buried and I had Duke to thank for that.

Duke

I wanted to be there for Gia, but I had my own business to attend to. I went to the hospital to see someone that I hadn't seen in a while. My heart hurt for Gia. She shouldn't have had to bury her sister so soon. That pain was one that I was all too familiar with.

I walked through the hospital contemplating on my life and where I would be had things been different. I made it out the hood, but it wasn't without help. My OGs were the ones that schooled me about everything but neither of them was able to witness my greatness. I was a king in the streets but what's a king without his queen? I was devoted and loyal to Gia whether she wanted me to be or not. I would do anything for her. *ANYTHING.*

When I walked into his room, I expected to see a corpse. I expected to see a man that was defeated. I expected to see remorse of some kind. When I walked into that room, I didn't see any of that. I saw a ruthless asshole who was fighting for a chance to prove himself. His name carried weight, but he had been gone from the game too long. He wasn't as careful as me and it showed.

"I didn't expect to see you here." He remarked as soon as he saw me.

"I didn't expect you to still be alive."

"Me either, cousin. What's going on with you?"

"I think that I'm gonna go to Tone's funeral in a few, but I came to check up on you. How you holdin' up?"

"Miserable as hell. I still can't believe that bitch nigga shot me."

"From my understanding and from what the news and multiple eye witnesses said…you shot him first. Tone was ready to make amends."

"Fuck him and his damn amends."

"Why is it that y'all were both selfish and stubborn as fuck but neither of you wanted to acknowledge that you were brothers?"

"I wanted his life and his dumb ass wanted mine. Our mama was a damn crackhead. Do you know how many times that bitch tried to sell me? Just for him to turn around and stab me in the back by setting me up. Now the feds on my ass because I can't give them a case to stay out of jail."

"Tyrek, you can't sit here and tell me that you don't feel no type of sadness. Your big brother is getting buried today."

"I heard. Grandma came to update me on everything. The doctors didn't think I was going to make it the other day. I had some sort of air embolism. They surprised that I made it."

"Damn."

"Yeah. She also told me that you paid for LaBrielle's funeral. Why?"

"I gotta have a reason to be a decent human?"

"Man cut the shit. You did that shit for a reason."

"Her sister. She's going through it pretty bad."

"Yeah. I bet." The sarcasm in Tyrek's voice irked me. He took my kindness for weakness any time I spoke of me doing something for someone I cared about.

"What? What's wrong with me helping her through a tough time?"

"Gia's sneaky as fuck. She probably the real reason behind Tone's hate. She a damn instigator. If it were up to me, that bitch would've been got dealt with. LaBrielle not in the picture no more so I might go ahead and do that."

"You touch her and you're gonna have to eat through a straw. I'm not playin' with you, Tyrek. She's off limits."

"Damn. You in love my nigga?" Tyrek sat up in his hospital bed and I crossed my arms. I thought that seeing how he was doing would be good for both of us; but truth be told, Tone was always my favorite cousin. His heart might as full of hate when it came to Tyrek but when it came to other shit, he was like me. We got along better. Tyrek was just a miserable asshole.

"I like her."

"You need to watch that lil bitch."

"Call her a bitch again." I uncrossed my arms, fists clenched. Tyrek laughed it off, but I was more than serious. No Gia slander was going to be tolerated, especially not around me.

"So, you really in love with that hoe? Damn lil cuz. Well, lemme tell you this. That lil pussy got power." Tyrek started laughing but before I knew it, I had my hands wrapped around his throat. I didn't even realize the heart monitors beeping rapidly.

"I TOLD YO BITCH ASS NOT TO TALK ABOUT HER LIKE THAT, DID I?!" Tyrek headbutted me and was able to catch his breath before I got myself back together and start punching his ass in the face.

"OH MY GOD! SECURITY!" A nurse called. She pulled me out of my trance, and I regained my composure. Tyrek was leaking but it wasn't bad enough to where he had any broken bones or needed stitches.

I walked out of Tyrek's room before security even had the chance to put their hands on me. The way I felt right now was dangerous. Tyrek had gotten under my skin and unleashed the beast that was inside. I knew that I was wrong for lashing out like that instead of walking away, but I couldn't help it.

I called Gia as soon as I got back to my car to let her know that I was going to meet up with her at the gravesite. I had to talk to her about Tyrek. I knew she wasn't a virgin by far, but I hadn't expected her to lay with someone like Tyrek's grimy ass. Tyrek wasn't worthy of entering her body. Hell, I wasn't even sure if I was worthy. *That's probably why she acts the way that she does.*

Gia

After awkward silence, it was nice to hear from Duke. I didn't think that I would want him around as much as I did. I'd never be able to admit that I cared about him. Duke was the type of man that didn't tell you that he would be there for you, he just showed you that he was the one.

When the funeral was over, I waited to see if Lyrik would show up. I knew that it was far-fetched, and my sister didn't exactly make anything easier. I felt bad for everything that happened.

"How long you been out here? It's hot as hell." Duke was walking up behind me in an all-black Armani suit. I smiled and rolled my eyes.

"Always got jokes." Duke grabbed me from behind and held me close. The feeling almost made me melt. Even worse, it made me break down my walls and shed a single tear. I wiped it away before he could see but I could feel the emotional transference.

"I knew this day would be hard on you. I'm sorry I wasn't there for you during the service but I'm here right now." I turned and looked Duke. "I mean it, Gia. I care about you. I got you." *Another tear…*

"Show me." Without warning, Duke kissed me. His arms wrapped around me and he damn near picked me up off the ground. The kiss was passionate yet gentle. When he finally pulled away, I noticed that his knuckles were bruised. "What happened to you?"

"I had something to deal with."

"If you want all of me, then you have to give me all of you." His sigh let me know that I should brace myself for whatever he was about to tell me.

"I went to see my cousin in the hospital."

"I thought your cousin was dead or is that a different cousin? Wait… You have a dead cousin and one that's dead?"

"Yeah." The confirmation made my heart drop.

"Tone and Tyrek."

"Gia –"

"Get away from me." I couldn't even look at Duke. I knew better. *You know better.*

"Gia, I know that LaBrielle and Tyrek had a past but –"

"Had a past?! He manipulated my sister into thinking that she couldn't live without him. And in the end, she believed it. My sister took her life for him. And how is he even alive? I thought Tyrek died in the hospital."

"No. He's fine. Well, he's decent. I just beat his ass for you."

"No. What you can do for me is kill that son of a bitch; cause I damn sure wouldn't hesitate to do it my damn self."

"Gia –"

"You lied to me!"

"I didn't lie."

"Nah, you just omitted the truth."

Chapter 6
Duke

Gia walked away from me and to her car. The thought of losing her caused me to shutter. It was obvious that I should've just been honest from the beginning, but I didn't want this to happen. Now, we were back to square one and Gia was going to have to see me in a vulnerable state before she trusted me again.

The only thing I could think to do was to go to my Aunt Patty's house to pay my respects for Tone's death. Between Gia and Tyrek, I didn't even make it to the funeral.

The more I thought about Gia's words, the more I wanted to go back to the hospital and finishing Tyrek's ass off. At this point, he was free game. He killed family. Tone was a grimy ass muthafucka just like Tyrek, but he didn't deserve death. Tone was no better than Tyrek. They were both hotheads who did a good job of fucking up my business with the catty little street wars that they frequently waged. Once Tyrek got out of the hospital, he wouldn't have a choice but to lay low due to the feds sniffing around.

With LaBrielle gone, he wouldn't dare attempt to go to Gia for help. Not when he was the cause of it. *But then again, this nigga got a silver tongue. He could charm the panties off a damn nun if he wanted to.* I could only hope that Gia didn't fall for any of his bullshit.

Claire

Since Tone's funeral, Miguel had been distancing himself from me. He hadn't been home as often, and his off days were spent at the gym and at his office. It almost seemed like he was avoiding me.

I was becoming paranoid. I loved Miguel, I truly did; but my heart belonged to Tone. I had always belonged to Tone, but I couldn't continue to be mistreated. I wanted a family with Tone but not it was too late.

I knew that Miguel was distancing himself because of my attitude for the past few days but I couldn't help but feel like Lyrik blabbed about my pregnancy. *What if she told him that the baby may not be his? What if it is?* I was at my breaking point with the secrecy.

I was sitting on the couch when Miguel came into the apartment. I heard him but I didn't dare look up from staring off into space. I was biting my lip and wondering whether or not I should say something. Miguel was a wonderful man, but I wasn't the woman for him. I was moody and in love with a dead man. I was damaged goods. A broken woman. No man deserved that type of baggage.

"Claire, we need to talk." The words that I was always afraid of. I instantly became anxious.

"About what?" Miguel walked up to the couch and sat by my side.

"Why you have been shutting me out lately? Is it because I told you about my daughters?

Do you not believe that I'm fighting for them?"

"Are you fighting for them, Miguel?"

"I didn't tell you because I didn't want to scare you. but I've been dealing with a custody battle for a while. We've been in and out of courts before I even met you. This isn't something new. I just didn't want you to become uninterested if you found out I had two children and a baby mama that isn't the nicest person in the world."

"So, when you had to run some errands to run…?"

"I was talking with lawyers. Trying to figure out what I could do next. My girls mean everything to me. Their young, they don't see everything just yet. They only see what she tells them, and I refuse to allow their mother to poison their minds." I assumed the worse out of the situation and that wasn't even the case. Miguel was doing everything to fight for his girls and I didn't even take the time to listen to him. I was used to the worst with Tone. *Maybe that's why I expected the worst.*

"Miguel, I'm sorry. I'm so sorry."

"I know. It's okay. I shouldn't blame you for your emotions." *He's perfect.* I couldn't help but to start bawling. Miguel didn't deserve this. "What's wrong?"

"I'm pregnant." Miguel's face perked up.

"That's a good thing. I love you and I'm here for you."

"The baby may not be yours…" I said it barely above a whisper, but even through my tears Miguel heard me loud and clear.

"Who else have you been with, Claire?"

"Before I moved in, before we made things official, I was still having sex with Tone every now and then."

"I can't believe this. This whole time you were mad at me for keeping secrets but you're no better!" Miguel got off the couch and walked out the door. I had no clue whether or not he would be back. The truth worried me.

Levi

I had been dreading talking about Nailah to Lyrik and Sahara. Lyrik had went through so much with her mother until I didn't even feel right about asking her to go see her mother. Lyrik had just gotten to a place of joy. Her internship at the hospital was over and she was going to graduate in a year's time. I didn't want anything to fall apart.

"Look, you have to give me time. You put those girls through hell. Especially Lyrik. You can't expect her to wait you around."

"I'm her mother. I know I did wrong. I know I did. Now, I'm trying to make things right." Nailah was crying and begging me to see Lyrik. I felt weird about keeping a mother from her child. Lyrik was my main concern.

"I'll talk to her today." I didn't want to, but I couldn't put off the inevitable. I kept sneaking off to meet with Nailah. Someone was bound to notice eventually. I had to suck it up and go ahead and talk to Lyrik about her mother.

Lyrik

Claire surprised me with her news. The thought of her having to tell Miguel that he might not be the father of her unborn child was heartbreaking. Miguel and Claire loved each other so I could only hope and pray that they worked through their issues. I had my own issues to deal with. I had been sitting on the toilet reading this pregnancy test box for at least ten minutes. I read it back and forth, up and down. Levi and I weren't always safe when I came to sex, but pregnancy never even crossed my mind. Neither of us were ready and Claire made me want to make sure that I was absolutely not pregnant.

"Plus sign means positive." I let out a long sigh then lifted the top of the toilet and pulled down my pants to pee on the stick. "Place on a dry surface and wait at least three minutes for results."

Playing the waiting game was not fun. One minute felt like an hour, three minutes felt like a lifetime. I cleaned myself up then washed my hands. I let out another sigh then looked at myself in the mirror. The 3-minute alarm on my phone went off. I took a deep breath then checked the test. *It's negative…*

A huge weight was lifted from my shoulders. I was not ready for a child. Truthfully, I didn't even know how to love. Levi had been teaching me how, but this was a job for my parents. My mother was an alcoholic and drug abuser and my father was M.I.A. I had no one to teach me about self-love and how to be treated. I had to teach myself about self-worth. I looked at myself in the mirror and couldn't believe that I was still here. I beat the odds.

"Lyrik, you home?!" Levi called from the front door.

"I'm in the bathroom! I'll be right out!" I hid any signs of a pregnancy test and exited the bathroom. But what I saw when I walked into the den was not something that I was expecting.

"So, this is what you've grown into. You're beautiful." My mother stood in front of me. Her frame was fragile but not deteriorating. She had kindness in her eyes. I had never seen an ounce of kindness in her before. "Let me take a look at you. Come here."

"Nailah, give her time." *Levi knew who she was? And still brought her here?* I felt a lump in my throat. I couldn't believe she was here. I didn't know whether I was sad or pissed. *Definitely pissed.*

"What are you doing here?"

"I begged Levi to let me see you. I've been going through my treatments. Sahara wants nothing to do with me. We went to her house first."

"You treated her like royalty compared to me. Did you honestly think that your reception would be anything less than hostile?"

"I know that I wasn't the best mother."

"You were the worst! You beat the fuck outta me on a daily basis!" I could taste the salt of the tears running down my face.

"And I'm sorry, Lyrik!"

"SORRY?!"

"Nailah, it's time to go." Levi had some nerve to even bring her before me. Nailah had been dead to me for years. I was forced to love her through the grace of God. but I never wanted her in my life again.

"No. She's gonna stay right here." Levi looked at me with a confused face but at this point, all I saw was red. All forgiveness that I thought I had in my heart disappeared.

"Lyrik…"

"Shut up!"

Levi

Lyrik was not the typical timid girl anymore. She spent countless years being abused by her mother. *I knew I shouldn't have done this shit.*

"Lyrik, calm down. Your mother isn't the same woman."

"I'm clean now, baby." Nailah pleaded. Lyrik didn't seem to care. Lyrik slapped Nailah across the face and caused her to fall and hit her head on the end of the coffee table. Blood was pouring from Nailah's head.

"Lyrik!"

"That bitch deserves that and so much more." Lyrik walked out of the room like her mother wasn't unconscious on the floor and bleeding out. I couldn't even begin to understand how she could do that, regardless of anything her mother did.

"Lyrik!" Lyrik was being extremely nonchalant about her mother slowly dying on our den floor; so, I picked up Nailah, placed her in my car, and drove her to the hospital myself. I hoped that Nailah made it in time but with the amount of blood she lost, I wasn't too sure.

Gia

After Duke told me about his connections to Tyrek and Tone, I expected for him to blow up my phone and ask for forgiveness. That wasn't the case. Duke didn't call me once. I wasn't sure whether I was mad because he didn't grovel for my forgiveness or because I actually wanted him to call.

I was looking at different apartments when he finally did call. I didn't know whether to ignore it or answer. Duke was different from other men that I've encountered, and I didn't want to risk him leaving out of my life permanently.

"Hello?"

I knew your mean ass was gon' answer. What you doin'?

"First of all, fuck you. Secondly, I'm looking for an apartment. I'm sick of living in that damn motel." *Bitch, why you sharing your plans with him?*

I been told you that you could stay at my place. I'm leaving back outta town soon anyway.

"What do you mean you leaving?" *Don't let him hear the hurt in your voice, don't let him see you sweat.*

I don't live down here no more. I gotta go back home and tend to my business. You thought I was playing when I said that I was hardly ever home?

"I mean…No, but –"

Look, meet me at the funeral home. I'm on my way there now. We can have this conversation then.

"Okay." And just like that he hung up. I craned my neck at the phone sitting in the passenger seat. *He really just hung up on me.* I felt like a little puppy. My man said come here and I just said 'yessir'.

I made my way to the funeral home on the other side of town. Duke had another thing coming if he thought that I would come running just because he said so. He already had waited almost a week before he called me but then he had the nerve to act like everything was all good. I was going over ways I was going to cuss him out in my head. Duke deserved every bit of my wrath. I went from wondering what I would say to wondering why I decided to wear a sundress with no panties. I chose the wrong day for that; especially dealing with a man like Duke. I just hoped that he wasn't on one today and he didn't try anything.

***

When I pulled up to the funeral home, Duke was already there leaning against his black BMW. His muscles were barely contained in the white V-neck shirt that he sported, and he was looking like a whole hoe in them damn grey sweatpants. His print was showing and he definitely wasn't a shrimp. He didn't even wait for me to put my car in park before he was tapping on my window and telling me to unlock the door. I complied and he got in the passenger seat. He looked basic but he was still fine as hell.

"What's been up with you?" Those pretty white teeth and that damn cologne.

"Really? You tell me you related to the muthafuckas that helped put my sister in the ground then you don't call—"

"So, you was waiting on me to call?"

"That ain't the fuckin' point, Maliek!"

"Damn. You gotta say my government name?"

"You damn skippy! You got some nerve—" Before I could even finish my sentence, Duke grabbed my head and pulled me in for a kiss. *I knew I should've changed clothes first.* The curls that I had in my hair had already began to fade away due to the heat and humidity, and now Duke was messing my hair up even more by grabbing a fist full of hair.

When we finally pulled away, Duke just stared into my eyes. My heart was pounding, and I didn't even understand why. I just knew that I felt differently about Duke than I had ever felt.

"Come get in my car." He ordered. I mindlessly did as I was told.

***

Duke drove for almost an hour until we were on the outskirts of town. *The suburbs...* Duke pulled into the driveway of one of the beautiful brick houses. And my jaw dropped at the size and architecture.

"Where are we?" I questioned. Duke put the car in park then turn off the ignition and got out. He ignored my question all together. I got out the car and followed.

The inside of the house was even more incredible. The grand staircase really made the foyer pop. I wasn't even paying attention to where Duke went. I just started walking around, hoping that I found him. I ended up in the kitchen and literally gawked at how beautiful everything was, but you could definitely tell that everything was for show. Nothing was stained, nothing looked used. Everything looked brand new.

"Uh-uh! Duke, who the fuck is this bitch?!" Some girl came through the other kitchen entrance and was yelling at the top of her lungs for Duke. My blood immediately started to boil. *Who the fuck is she?* Duke came running and immediately started apologizing to me.

"I'm sorry. Jazmine, this is Gia. Gia, this is my dumbass sister Jazmine." Duke looked like he was ready to smack the shit out of Jazmine.

"Half-sister. I wouldn't dare come from your daddy. That whole side of the family crazy as hell."

"Why the fuck are you even in my house?" Duke asked through clenched teeth.

"You don't be here, and I wanted to use the jacuzzi tub. Sis need a nice lil getaway, but I see you and your bitch finna—" Duke hemmed Jazmine's ass up fast as hell.

"Don't call her outta her name. Next time you do, I won't hesitate to put you in your place. I don't care if you are my sister. She's my woman. I will make your ass disappear. Do you understand me?" He didn't raise his voice one time and she was shaking. All Jazmine could do was nod. I never had someone defend me some fiercely. *Bitch, I know you ain't falling in love.*

"I'm sorry. I'll leave." Jazmine damn near ran for the exit. I had to stifle my laughter when her ass almost fell.

"So, I guess the Bentley outside wasn't yours?"

"The red Continental GT was hers. I have a black one in the garage. A Coupe. Matter of fact, come with me."

I followed closely behind Duke as he led me towards the garage. He turned on the lights and I damn near lost my breath. He had a four-car garage and none of the cars in the garage looked anything less that expensive as hell.

"Damn." Was all I could allow myself to say.

"Pick one out."

"Pick one out?" Duke smiled at my reaction. I blushed.

"Yeah, pick one out. Which one you like more?"

"I don't know. All of them are nice and definitely out of my price range."

"Don't worry about all that. Which one do you like more?"

"I don't know. The grey one at the far end?"

"Okay. Here." Duke handed me a set of keys.

"Um…What is this?"

"Well, that key is a key to the house. That key is a key to that 2019 Tesla that you just picked out."

"Wait, what?!" *Did he just give me a damn car and the key to his house?*

"I don't know why you surprised. My woman wants for nothing and I handle all of her needs."

"Duke, I can't accept this. Any of this." *Yes, you can!* My inner thoughts were battling it out over this man. I wanted him then I didn't then I did again.

"This car goes from 0 to 60 in less than 5 seconds. It—"

"That's nice but I can't accept it. I probably couldn't even begin to pay for it."

"It's paid for. I don't do car notes." Duke laughed.

"Is it stolen?"

"No. I don't need to steal what I could easily afford."

"How much is the car, Duke?"

"Before customizing it? About $176,000."

"Before customizing—Are you crazy?"

"No. I can afford it. Just trust me."

"Trust you? No low-level drug dealer is pulling in that kinda money. This is beyond that. What do you do?"

"I told you that already."

"No. You only told me what you thought I wanted to hear."

"I bring things into the United States. I get paid handsomely. The end."

"So, you're a mule?"

"I don't just deal with drugs."

"Do you deal with sex trafficking or anything like that?"

"No. The opportunity has presented itself, but I am a man of morals and virtue. I turned the offer down countless times. I like money but not that much. I do, however, smuggle in immigrants who want to make a better life for themselves. We smuggle them in and give them the tools necessary to become a legal citizen."

"How much does that pay?" Duke looked at me like he was offended.

"You don't put a price on someone's freedom. I put outta pocket to make sure that they have a great start when they get here. I build houses, I give them affordable cars, I give them jobs at my fronts. We pay a great deal to much sure that they aren't struggling when they do become citizens. It's more of a charitable act. I don't like the thought of someone being denied the freedoms that I enjoy. Simple." I looked at Duke in a totally different light.

"That's admirable." Duke's serious face melted into a small smirk as he looked down at his feet.

"Thank you."

When he looked at me, I felt butterflies. He was a man that showed his affections more than just telling me the obvious shit that I wanted to hear. He leaned in for a kiss and I obliged. Duke picked me up in his strong arms and carried me to the master bedroom. I laughed the entire way up the stairs.

"This is beautiful."

"Now, it's yours."

"I guess that means that you're still leaving."

"Unless I have a reason to stay."

"Am I not reason enough to stay?" I turned towards Duke and he grabbed me and pulled me in close. He kissed me more passionately than he ever had before. When he pulled away, he pulled off his shirt and threw me on the bed. He laid on top of me and continued to kiss me like he'd never see me again. He started to hike up my sundress and stopped when he reached the top of my thigh.

"We shouldn't be doing this."

"Wait what?"

"I want you to give yourself to me. Not the other way around."

"Are you kidding me right now?"

"I care about you. Your heart is fragile. I don't wanna do the wrong thing and break it." *A man, a king.*

I ignored all of Duke's warnings. If something happened, then we'd deal with it then. I undid his pants and pulled off my sundress. Duke looked at me like he was starving, and I was 5 course meal. He ripped off my bra and took his time kissing every inch of me. From my lips to my collarbone. Duke took his time to tease me and leave me wanting more. The way he licked and gentle nibbled on my nipple caused them to become erect. He continued to cup my breast as he moved further down with his kisses. He reached my stomach and made circles around my navel. My breathing became more rigid. Duke moved lower and began kissing on the inside of my thighs.

"You better stop teasing me." I was growing impatient, but Duke made sure I knew who was in charge.

"You wanted this. So, I'm gonna take my time."

Duke made circular motions with his tongue around my pearl but never touched it outright. I tried to catch him off guard and thrust my hips forward, but he grabbed my thighs and pinned me to the bed. He let out a low growl and began deep sea diving into my ocean. I arched my back and tried to pull away after climaxing multiple times. Duke gripped my thighs tighter and refused to turn me loose. I could've sworn I saw my soul leave my body by the time he finished his meal. Duke wasted no time and slowly slid himself into me and I gasped. He wasn't my first but he was definitely the biggest. He heard my gasp and decided to go slowly until I was more comfortable with his length.

The moaning and grunting between us two sounded like a symphony. His strokes getting deeper and faster with each stroke. I tried to moan but the deeper he went, the harder it was for words to come out. Duke was gentle, passionate at first; but he soon turned into a savage. I arched my back and Duke pulled me into his lap with ease. I matched his rhythm and continued to ride him until we switched positions. The lust we felt for each other had boiled over and us having sex for two hours proved it. He grabbed my hair; I bit my lip. He gave me back shots while I arched my back and moaned. I couldn't grip the sheets tight enough. When he smacked me on my ass, I knew that I was in over my head. Duke was nowhere near done and I stopped counting my orgasms after the third one. He clearly was more experienced that anyone that I have ever been with and he listened to my body language.

"I thought this is what you wanted? Don't run." Duke smacked my ass and I was damn near dying from yet another orgasm. This man was about to sex me to death. I wanted to stop because I was scared of getting dehydrated but on the other hand if it was my time to go then this would definitely be the best way to go. Duke pulled my hair and was kissing all over my neck. I could feel myself becoming sore. Duke had a point to prove and I was going to let him.

Chapter 7
Duke

I was trying to take things easy on Gia, but she was tantalizing to me. One minute, she wanted to be around me and the next… I didn't want her to experience how rough I could be. I wanted our first time to be gentle and romantic, but it turned into a damn brawl. I knew that she was going to be a problem. I pulled her hair and she made the sexiest moan. I was trying to hold on, but I couldn't even do it anymore. I bust deep inside of her and neither of us even seemed to care.

I continued to lay on her back and play with her hair. Tyrek was still on my mind with the things that he said about Gia. After having her after wanting her for a while, I had to get to the truth about her relationship with

Tyrek. I knew that asking her was probably going to ruin the mood, so I just didn't bother. I got up to go to the bathroom and Gia followed. I even washed her hair while we were both in the shower. We both remained silent. The smile on her face let me know that her inner thoughts were probably running wild. I didn't even reveal my full potential and she was acting differently. I didn't have to work as hard to make her smile.

***

After the shower, I showed Gia to the closet where I had clothes picked out for her. She decided to wear a black bra and panty set and a navy Champions tracksuit. The tracksuit hugged her curves and I was damn near ready for another round. I watched her put her hair in a messy bun as I put on my own clothes. She looked perfect sitting with her legs crossed on my bed. I hadn't even noticed that I was just straight up staring at her until she looked up from her phone.

"Why you staring at me like that?" Gia was blushing hard as hell. I couldn't do nothing but smile. That was my woman right there.

"Just thinking about a few things." I put my black wife beater on and walked towards her. She seemed to brace herself for my next move.

"Thinking about what?" Tyrek instantly popped into my head and I tried to keep my composure, but she could see that something was wrong. "Just tell me."

"What happened between you and Tyrek?"

"What?"

"What happened between you and Tyrek?"

"He dated my sister."

"That's not what I meant, and you know damn well that ain't what I meant."

"Duke, I—"

"So, y'all did fuck?"

"He was my first. I thought he cared about me."

"He was dating your sister! Openly!"

"I know. I know that, okay?" Gia started crying and I instantly fell back.

"Look, I just wanted to know the truth before we moved forward. He said some shit about you that fucked with me." I sat down on the bed next to her and tried to console her.

"I guess that he told you about Tone too, huh?" The comforting hug that I had Gia wrapped in instantly got tighter.

"What happened with Tone?"

Gia

Damn. I should've kept my mouth closed. Duke held me so tight until I could tell that he was already hurt by my words.

"I didn't want to say anything, but me and Tone used to creep around. It wasn't anything serious."

"Honestly, I can't even get mad. All that was before me and you didn't even know me back then. Just know that you ain't finna be out here doing whoever or whatever you want. You my woman now. I expect nothing less than loyalty and you'll receive the same in return." *What in the hell?*

"So, you're not mad?"

"No." I hadn't even realized that Duke's grip on me had loosened.

"Do you feel less of me?"

"For being single and doing single shit? No. It might have been foul, but that shit ain't have shit to do with me. As long as you clean, we good."

"I get checked every three months and I know how to use condoms. You're the only person, I didn't use a condom with."

"How many people you been with?"

"Three. My body count not high. How bodies you done caught? Yo stroke game was way to precise."

"Believe it or not, I've only been with three women before you. The first two were a hit it and quit type situation. The one before you, I was with her for years. She was older but she taught my young ass a few tricks."

"You like them old bitches, huh?" Duke and I laughed, and he kissed my forehead.

"I like you." He bit his lip and I couldn't help but bite mine too. Duke was flat out gorgeous. Just from looking at him, you wouldn't think that he was a drug dealer. Duke invested his money wisely and had built two separate empires.

"I got a question."

"Speak on it."

"Why didn't you put Tyrek and Tone on when you made it big?"

"I tried, but they were more into the physical aspects of the game. Starting wars with other drug dealers and shit is bad for business. I told them to knock that shit off, they wouldn't listen. They put me in the game, but my intellect and determination helped me rise above them." Duke shrugged then looked at me like he was waiting for another question.

"What you lookin' at me like that for? You expecting me to interview you or something?"

"You been doing that. You had lots of questions, I just wanted to answer all your questions."

"Okay. Since we playin' 21 questions and shit… What made me wanna talk to me? What made you approach me?"

"I always had a small crush on you when we were kids, but then I left. When I came back, you blossomed. You were different."

"Kids? I don't remember you."

"Yeah. I know. I wasn't exactly the man you see today. I was extra skinny, braces, thick ass glasses… We were in the same 5th grade class, but you were always beautiful to me." Duke's response sent a chill up my spine. *Why didn't I notice him before?* I could've been living in this fairy tale, but I guess everything happens for a reason. I just hoped that Duke didn't switch up on me like the "men" in my past.

Claire

Miguel and I hadn't spoken in weeks and he hadn't been home. He was ignoring all my calls and texts. I sent him a text to let him know about my doctor's appointment. If he showed, then I knew that there was a chance and he still cared; if he didn't show, then there was no chance in hell that I would get him back. I just hoped that I wasn't going to be alone at that doctor's office.

***

I sat in the waiting area for no more than 15 minutes before they called me to the back. I was nervous until Miguel walked into the waiting area. I called him over and he walked with me to the back.

"Thank you for coming." I whispered.

"I just want to make sure that the baby that could possibly be mine is okay." The venom in his voice made me feel like shit. I didn't deserve it…or maybe I did.

The nurse ushered us into a room where she would check the baby's heartbeat and to see how the baby was developing.

"We'll be right with you okay?" I nodded. Miguel sat on a nearby stool in silence as I paced around the room. He didn't even look at me. He was on his phone the whole time.

"Miguel, can you please talk to me?"

"For what? So that you can accuse me of something else? So that you can act like I mean nothing to you? You treated me like I was nothing and now you want me to acknowledge you?"

"I'm sorry. I know that I was mean and I –"

"Mean? No. You were a bitch to me. And you accused me of not caring for my kids. You can go to the depths of Hell." *Ouch.*

"I deserve your anger. I know that you're upset, but I don't deserve to be spoken to like that. Like I'm lower than trash."

"You don't even know who your child's father is."

"Why are you like this?"

"Okay, how are you guys doing today?" The doctor came in and interrupted our discussion.

"We're fine." Miguel answered coldly.

"Let's see if we can hear a heartbeat. Come sit up here." I made my way to the hospital bed for a check-up. The doctor lifted my shirt and began to check for a heartbeat but heard nothing.

"Is something wrong?" I began to panic as the doctor continued to roam around my stomach to look for the baby.

"I don't see a baby in here. Your lab results show as pregnant, but I don't see a baby." The doctor wiped the cold gelatin off my stomach and sighed.

"Well, how is that possible?" Miguel was unclenching a little and his concern made me feel a little better.

"Have you taken any new prescriptions or medications before your pregnancy diagnosis?"

"The only thing that I've taken before I found out were some weight loss pills. I felt I was gaining weight and bought some weight loss pills. I didn't react well to them and threw up but then I just kept throwing up. I took a test and it said positive."

"Weight loss pills? Do you remember the name?"

"No. All I remember is them starting with an 'H'."

"Human chorionic gonadotropin or hCG?"

"Yeah." The expression on the doctor's face was more than enough for me to start panicking and hyperventilating.

"What does that mean? She was never pregnant?" Miguel broke the silence and his words felt somewhat like a relief.

"No. She was never pregnant. Human chorionic gonadotropin is a hormone in pregnant women, but it can also be used in weight loss. You experienced pregnancy side effects due to this hormone. The irritability and mood swings, bloating, swelling of feet, vomiting – all side effects."

"But I haven't had a period in over a month."

"Stress. This was a very traumatic time for you and the news of a possible baby just made it worse. When your stress levels go down, your cycle will come on. I don't want you doing any strenuous activities, okay?" I nodded my head and the doctor left the room. I couldn't believe that all this time, I thought that I was pregnant, and I really wasn't. I looked over at Miguel. My eyesight was misty, and I could feel my tears staining my face. Miguel didn't really have any emotion on his face.

"I'm not pregnant." I whispered. Miguel looked at me but still remained emotionless.

"I need some time apart. I just need to see if this is what I want."

"Miguel—"

"You're younger than I am. Live your life. Make mistakes. But I don't know if I want to be a part of that."

"But I love you."

"But you are in love with someone I can never be." Miguel walked out of the room and I broke down. I thought that I knew everything and now two men that I loved were no longer in my life. I could only hope that Miguel came around.

Lyrik

I had been avoiding Levi for weeks. It got to the point where I started back sleeping in my old room instead of the room that we shared. Levi had no right to bring my mother to the house. He took her to the hospital after she hit her head. When he got back home, he was telling me how she was going to be okay and how sorry he was. I didn't care to hear any of that. I loved Levi to the depths of my soul, but I refused to be around that woman.

Today was a rare occasion in which Levi didn't have to work. He rarely had off days anymore. When he walked in the kitchen, I wanted to walk back out, but he grabbed my arm.

"You can't keep avoiding me."

"I can't?" I snatched my arm back and went to the refrigerator. I could feel Levi standing behind me. I grabbed the yogurt from the bottom shelf and closed the door. I walked around Levi and sat down at the island in our kitchen.

"You can't be this full of hatred. All the times you told me that you forgave your mother…"

"You're right. I'm a hypocrite. I thought that I was over it but when I looked at her, all I wanted to do was stomp her ass out. I wanted her to suffer, to bleed out half to death. Like how she did me. You weren't there that night. Sahara saved my life. I would've died that night. I don't fault you for leaving and choosing a better life, but bringing her here?"

"I overstepped my boundaries. You right, but I'm not about to let you shut me out." I rolled my eyes and continued to eat my yogurt. When I felt it coming back up, I ran to the bathroom and threw up until I was dry heaving into the toilet. Levi grabbed my hair and allowed me to vomit freely without any getting into my hair.

"You okay?"

"Yeah"

"You coming down with a virus or something? You been sick for a minute."

"Just because I've been sick doesn't mean that I have a virus."

"You need to stop being stubborn and go to the hospital. You can't keep food down."

"Boy, fuck you." I flushed the toilet and went to the sink to brush my teeth. Levi trailed me like a puppy.

"You can be mad at me all you want but I'm calling a doctor." I rolled my eyes and Levi helped me into my bed. I didn't want his assistance, but I was too fragile to even argue or turn down his help.

***

Dr. Franklin made her way to the house on short notice. Levi had made it clear that I was to be taken care of and watched while he ran some errands. I felt helpless and having to rely on Levi made me feel even worse. I didn't feel like dealing with his definition of "care".

"Is there a possibility that you could be pregnant?" Dr. Franklin asked.

"No. I took a test a few weeks ago and it was negative."

"I want to run a few tests. I going to take a few blood samples, a urine test and I'm going to check your vitals. All that jazz. I'm going to make sure that you feel better, okay?" I was annoyed at everything at this point. Levi was trying to force a relationship between me and my mother. I knew that I deserved a normal relationship with my mother, but I had to do it on my own terms.

Dr. Franklin wasted no time escorting me to the bathroom so that I could do my urine test. After I peed and flushed the toilet, I was back on my knees and throwing up nothing but liquids. At this point, it was hard to keep anything down and I was sick of it. I had thrown up so much until I was literally nothing left. Dr. Franklin helped me back to my bed and checked my vitals.

"We have to get some food in your system. You look borderline dehydrated. When was the last time you were able to keep down food?"

"A bout two weeks, maybe more."

"And you're just not seeking medical attention?"

"I had a fever. I figured it was the flu. They make medicine for the flu and I don't need a doctor to tell me what I already know." Dr. Franklin's watch started ringing then she went back into the bathroom. I sighed and was about to pass out when she came back into the room with a Cheshire Cat grin on her face. "What?"

"Congratulations. You're pregnant." Dr. Franklin held up three pregnancy tests from my urine sample and I fainted.

Levi

Lyrik had been avoiding me like the plague. She wanted no parts of being with me and I didn't blame her. When I got a text from Nailah during Dr. Franklin's house call, I knew that I had to see how she was doing. I also took the opportunity to go and see Tyrek. He was supposedly going to be dispatched soon. I couldn't miss the opportunity to see him.

When I walked into his room, he sat up in his bed. He was watching tv, but his attention turned to me. He smiled. Almost like he knew I'd come and see him eventually.

"Baby bro, what took so long? Lyrik must got you on a tight leash."

"At least I have Lyrik. That must severely both you. The fact that our mom gave me and Tone a better life by giving us up, but you – you were abused in every way imaginable. Tone envied you because you had the chance to know our mother. But I knew the truth. That woman was not worthy of being a mother to anyone. She turned you into a monster."

"When did you find out about me and Tone? Why you never said nothing?"

"I didn't care. I had a family already. I didn't need the approval of another one. Less of all, you. Tone was cool with me and I love our Grandma, but you? You could rot in hell for all I care."

"Damn. So, the middle child is really the black sheep, huh?"

"You could be on fire and I would use rubbing alcohol to put you out. Do yourself a favor and stay away from me and Lyrik."

"Oh... I see. She doesn't know about your little secret, huh? What do you think would happen if she were to find out?"

"If you come near her ever again, I will personally make sure that you never take another breath again."

"That's cold."

"And you look like shit. Who beat your ass this time?"

"Cousin Duke. Apparently, he has a thing for LaBrielle's little sister. I brought her up and he went ape shit."

"You would think that all that time you spent fighting crackhead would've gave you better fighting skills." Tyrek laughed as I walked out of the room. I had disowned him the moment I found out about him years ago. That was part of the real reason I left. Lyrik was in a relationship with Tyrek and I was mad at the world. I was mad at her. She didn't know the truth, but I did. I was more than happy to find out that I was her first and she wasn't tainted by Tyrek misguided view of how love was supposed to be. I visited Nailah but I didn't stay long. Dr. Franklin sent me a text saying that she was coming to the hospital with Lyrik.

Duke

Gia and I truly had a love/hate relationship. When we were good, everything was good; when we were bad, we were at war. The love that I had for her never wavered. The arguing was petty and sometimes redundant, but I knew that I had to teach her how to love properly if I wanted to be with her. Gia was a gentle creature and I couldn't even begin to understand how anyone could do her wrong. I couldn't imagine why she wasn't a wife yet. I never understood the caution that she displayed whenever she spoke to me; but bit by bit, I was breaking down all of her walls and barriers.

As Gia rested her head on my chest, I played with her hair. She was more angelic when she was asleep. I kissed her forehead and her eyes started to flutter.

"I'm sorry. I didn't mean to wake you." I whispered.

"It's okay." Her doe like eyes and her beautiful grin… I could see the love that she had for me.

"Since you're up. I got something that I have to ask you." She furrowed her brows and gave me the cutest, stank face ever.

"What?" Gia sat up in the bed and held the covers up to her chest to keep from exposing herself. I reached over into the top nightstand drawer and I pulled out a black box with a red ribbon. Gia looked at me then looked at the box. I smiled at her expression and handed her the box.

"Open it." She slowly pulled the ribbon off the box and took a deep breath. When she opened the box, she gasped and covered her mouth with her hand.

"Maliek..." She was the only person that I allowed to call me by my government name. I could see the tears glistening in her eyes.

"I just wanted to show you how I felt about you. We may fuss and fight, we may not always agree, but I love you and I would love to be in your life for forever and a day. If you'll have me that is."

"You don't think that we may be moving a little fast?"

"I know what I want. I know who I want. I showed you how I felt. The ball is in your court now." I kissed Gia on the forehead and got up to take a shower. She just gawked at the custom diamond ring that was in her hand. Something inside of me hoped that she would say yes but I knew that Gia was too full of pride to accept outright. She was going to need to be coaxed. I just hoped that she wasn't thinking about the situation too deeply.

Chapter 8
Gia

I had damn near moved in with Duke, but I didn't expect that he was falling for me. He showed me how I was supposed to be treated but he was still secretive at times. I wasn't sure if I could trust him enough for marriage. I had to basically force him to tell me about his occupation and the reality of it. But I still knew little about how everything was run, who worked for him, or who he worked for. Someone with dark intentions could come to the house one day and say that they worked for Duke and I would be forced to believe them. I didn't want to put my trust into someone who still couldn't tell me everything.

I was truly grateful for everything that Duke had done for me. He popped into my life when I was dealing with some deep shit and pulling me to the other side. LaBrielle was on my mind daily. Although I loved Duke and I told him that I forgave him for keeping his family ties a secret, his secrets continued to make me doubt his authenticity.

I looked at the ring that Duke had just given me and felt a rush of mixed emotions. When my cellphone rang, I was glad to be awakened from the hypnotic trance that it had me in. That is until I realized that Tyrek was the one calling my phone. I had been trying to figure out how I was going to finish him off since the original plan didn't work. He was like a roach. He could have a nuclear bomb dropped on his ass and he would still be alive. I ignored the first call but after the second, third and fourth, I figured that I should just answer the phone.

"What?"

Damn. Is that any way to treat the love of your life? I just got out of the hospital. They told me that you came to visit almost every day.

"I wanted to make sure that you were dead from your wounds. Clearly, that is not the case."

So, you wished bad on me? I wonder how Duke would feel about his girl—

"Yo, real talk, just shut the fuck up and don't call my fuckin' phone again unless you ready to lose your fuckin' life. You deadass crackin' jokes like my sister isn't dead. My sister killed herself because she couldn't live without you and you out here alive and still on the fuck shit. Bye, Tyrek." I hung up the phone and hadn't noticed that Duke was standing in the door listening to my conversation. He had his arms folded with a sly ass grin on his face. "What?"

"Nothing." He tried to hide his smile but was unsuccessful.

"Nah, what you cheesin' for?"

"Nothing. Got put some clothes on. We got a flight to catch." *'A flight to catch'?*

Claire

Miguel made it clear that until I could get myself together, then I didn't need to be in a relationship...or at least not one with him. He allowed me to stay at the apartment until I could find somewhere else to stay. The entire situation was making me feel like shit. Luckily, I did have a place to move to. The apartment that I shared with Tone.

The rent was already paid up for the rest of the year that Tone and my name were on the lease. After that, either I renewed the lease or moved out. Being back in such a dark place was not what I had in mind, but I had to go somewhere.

I had never experienced life before. I was young when I got with Tone and I got with Miguel soon after. The only friend I had was

Lyrik and she was going through her own shit with Levi.

I decided that I should just go out solo. I needed a drink and I wasn't about to stay in the house just because everybody else was unavailable.

I put on my best little black dress and did my hair. I decided to literally let my hair down.

***

I pulled up to the club and instantly felt back in my element. I hadn't been to a club or party since the night that Tone died. I was ready to turn up. No commitments, no strings attached. Shot after shot and the first thought that came to my mind wasn't Tone, it was Miguel. I thought that I would be able to get over Miguel but as the night went on, as I sat at the bar getting drunk as hell, I realized that I wanted Miguel and I wasn't going to stop until he was mine.

I know that I shouldn't have driven from the club, but I couldn't help it. I had to get to Miguel to let him know how I felt. I was swerving through traffic. Miguel had to know how I felt.

HOOOOONNNNKKK!

Cars were blowing at me as I continued to the direction of Miguel's house. I drove through red lights, I bypassed cars without any worry. Deep inside, I knew that I should be more careful than what I actually was. I knew that if the cops were to catch me, then I would end up in jail for a DUI. I didn't care. Miguel was my only concern. I was ready to put everything on the line for him.

CRASH!

Lyrik

Dr. Franklin stayed with me the entire time that I was being admitted into the hospital. I didn't know what to feel. I was out for a while then when I came to, I started to hyperventilate. I was in panic mode and all the doctors in my room. *I'm pregnant? How did this happen? When did this happen?*

"Lyrik, you need to calm down and breathe, sweetie." Dr. Franklin directed. I tried to get my breathing under control and was able to succeed after a few minutes. My breathing went back to normal and my vitals were checked yet again to make sure nothing happened to me or the baby during my fainting spell. Levi came into the room and was asking questions immediately. I didn't want to see him, but I knew that I would have to tell him the truth.

"What's going on?" Levi was frantic. There was no doubt in my mind that he cared for me. A blind man could see the love that he had for me. I don't know why I questioned it so much. What Levi did was fucked up, but his intentions were good. *He was just trying to make me happy. Why was I punishing him for trying to make me happy?*

"She's alright. She just fainted. We're just making sure that there no alternative reason for her fainting, other than the dehydration and shock."

"Dehydration? Shock?"

"I think she should tell you the news herself." Dr. Franklin tried to contain her smile then looked between me and Levi before she left the room.

Levi sat beside my hospital bed and grabbed my right hand. He kissed the back of my hand and looked like he was praying over me silently to himself. *This is the man that you're mad at. This is the man that you've been shunning these past few weeks.*

"Levi…"

"Don't talk. Save your energy."

"Levi, I'm fine. I just fainted."

"She said shock and dehydration. That means that you need to rest. And we have to get some liquids in you."

"I'm already juiced up." I mumbled under my breath. Levi looked at me confused as hell.

"What?!"

"I'm pregnant, Levi." Levi shot up and grabbed me. He kissed me all over. Safe to say that he was happy about me being pregnant.

"This is amazing news. Why don't you seem happy?"

"Because I'm not. I'm scared, worried. I had a mother that would beat my ass and now she wants to be a mother. She wants to right all of her wrongs. Why would I want to be a mother just so that I could possibly mimic what I saw growing up?"

"You saw that and now you know how to not to be. Just because Nailah was a horrible mother, doesn't mean that you will. You can't just assume the worst."

"I can't? I thought that when I started having kids that I would be married and finished with school."

"1 out of 2 isn't too bad is it?" I rolled my eyes and sighed.

"What are you talking about? I'm still in school and we aren't married."

"Not yet." Levi pulled a box out of his pants and placed it in my lap. I held the box in my hands and caressed the velvet box. When I opened the box, the marquise shaped diamond sparkled in the light of the sun shining through the hospital window.

"Levi, it's beautiful but I can't accept this." As much as I would've loved to wear this ring, I just couldn't get over Levi talking to my mother behind my back. Levi looked like he had just lost his best friend and the truth of the situation was that…he did.

Duke

Gia was solid as hell and I felt the need to show her just how much I trusted her. I had her pack a few bags so that we could leave town. I was going for business but bringing Gia along would definitely add some pleasure. I had my driver pick us up and Gia looked shocked at the old black man that was driving the Rolls Royce.

"Who is that?" Gia was hesitant to get in the car.

"Do you trust me?" Gia smacked her lips and rolled her eyes.

"Yeah."

"Then get in before we miss our flight." *She rolls her eyes at me again and I'm gonna fuck her so hard they stay in that position...*

***

When we arrived at the airport, everyone was waiting at the jet to greet us. I could tell that Gia was pleased but slightly uncomfortable. The fact that nobody was able to provide her with this kind of lifestyle made me want to go even harder to spoil her. The next man after me was going to have problems out the ass if he came with anything less than what I could provide. I gave to Gia freely with no strings attached. I wanted her heart, but I let her give it to me on her own terms.

"All of this is yours?" Gia asked as we both exited the Rolls Royce. I could hear the discomfort in her voice.

"Yes. Just remember: What's mines is yours." I kissed her reassuringly on the forehead and we walked towards the jet.

"Good morning, Mr. Williams. Complimentary mimosas?"

Gia reluctantly took one of the champagne flukes off of the serving tray.

"We hope you enjoy your flight." The stewardess followed us aboard the plane and helped us to our seats.

***

"You okay?" Gia was silent, staring out the window. She didn't say much of anything since we boarded. She bit her bottom lip and I went crazy. She looked so cute when she was nervous.

"Just thinking. Where we going, Maliek?"

"You know you can call me 'Duke', right?" Gia chuckled softly and brushed her hair out of her face and behind her ear. She hadn't worn weave in the past month or so of us knowing each other. I've offered but that was one thing that she refused to let me do for her. Instead, she just wore her real hair. It wasn't like her real hair wasn't long and beautiful. She was natural but she rarely wore it in its curly state. She preferred to blow it out or wear it completely straight.

"Whatever. Answer the question."

"Emilio wanted to meet with me. Originally, I told him 'no' because I was with you. I told him about how you come first. He invited you along."

"Wait…This is a business trip? Why would you bring me?!"

"He invited you. Plus, Emilio is like a father figure. I never even mentioned a woman in his presence. You would be the first woman that I've ever dealt with to meet him." Gia tensed up even more at the thought of meeting my boss. The man that was more of a father to me than my own father. I couldn't blame her; I just hoped that she kept herself together.

Gia

I know that I asked about Duke's operation, but I didn't think he would comply. Taking me to meet Emilio before I met his workers was a major move. He expected me to be around for the long haul. I wasn't just some passing fling.

The plane began to descend and the palm trees in the distance welcomed us with open arms. Duke had let me know that this island was off the coast of Mexico. Everything looked so beautiful and different. A black man in a white linen suit was waiting for us outside of the plane. I couldn't see his face through the plane window before he started talking to someone in the opposite direction.

"Ready?" Duke snapped me out of my thoughts. I nodded and he grabbed my hand to help me to my feet.

We exited the plane and I could feel my stomach in knots. My palms were getting clammy. I knew that Duke could sense my anxiety by the way he kissed the back of my hand. I calmed down only slightly. The closer we got to Emilio the more I felt like I would vomit.

"Emilio, this is Gia. Gia, this is Emilio." When Emilio turned around, my eyes began to swell with tears. I couldn't even begin to understand how I felt. I flurry of emotions surrounded me. Duke was talking but I couldn't hear him. My eyes were locked onto Emilio. He looked at me with confusion. *He doesn't even know who I am… He doesn't remember me.*

The main emotion that I felt was anger. He clearly didn't remember me. The tears in my eyes that I tried to hold onto began to fall like a waterfall. I couldn't hide behind a mask anymore. The source of the hurt that I tried so hard to forget about, that I tried so hard to ignore, was standing right in front of me. My father that left my mother high and dry to wither away was standing in front of me. The man that left and made a family with someone new… I had wanted to keep in touch but after a few years he stopped visiting and writing letters.

He stopped being a father to me and he devoted all of his time to his new family. I was a distant memory and it showed. He didn't even recognize my face. Duke was continuously trying to figure out why I was having a complete breakdown. Emilio still didn't understand what was happening.

Before I realized what I was doing, I cocked back and delivered a vicious right hook. Emilio staggered backwards and revealed the blood that began to spout from his nose.

Duke held me back as I kicked and screamed. I was acting like a pissed off toddler having a temper tantrum. All of the hurt that I held inside of me for the past 10 to 15 years, was finally being released. Emilio barked orders to have me killed and Duke continuously apologized on my behalf.

"Yo! This ain't like her! What the fuck happened between y'all?!"

"I don't know the bitch!" *Bitch? Bitch?! I'll show you a bitch!*

I struggled to Duke's strength. He was not about to let me go and he wasn't about to let Emilio dispose of me either. I struggled to be free, but I couldn't get out of Duke's vise-like grip. I eventually stopped trying to break free and like began to wail. I never cried so deeply in my life. Duke had never seen me this vulnerable, he had never seen me this emotional. My entire body went limp and Duke continued to hold me. Emilio ordered Duke to take me to our room that we were supposed to be occupying and to tend to me.

Apparently, Duke had plead with Emilio enough for Emilio to spare my life for violating him the way that I did. I couldn't imagine the pain that I potentially caused Duke. I was so wrapped up in my own issues, until I didn't even think about Duke's feelings. This man was the one that Duke considered a second father. His second father just so happened to be my biological father.

Duke

I had never seen Gia lose control like that. Even when she lost her sister, Gia managed to keep it together to an extent. Her snapping like that caused me to think that she had a relationship with Emilio. Whether he wanted to admit it or not. He frequently visited our hometown under a different name, it's only logical that he might have seduced her a time or two. I didn't want to think of the man I considered my father and my woman in that light, but that was the only logical explanation that I could think of.

"Your girl packs a mean punch." Emilio wasn't prone to mercy and sympathy; so, asking him to spare Gia's life was a stretch. Him actually accepting my request was out of his love for me. I was the son that he wished that I had. Emilio poured himself and me some scotch and began to pace his office.

"I'm sorry about that, G. I don't know what got into her." I took a sip of the amber color liquid and let the hot and cold sensation take over.

"Women are emotional creatures. Just make sure that she doesn't try that shit again. I love you like you were my own son, but I be damned if I let anybody disrespect me on my own damn island."

"Understood. You know her?"

"Hell no. I'm just as confused as you are."

I could see that Emilio was genuinely confused, but Gia reacted out of pure anger.

That kind of anger was lingering. I knew from experience that that type of anger was from a past filled with hurt.

"I gotta talk to her. Maybe I can figure out what's wrong."

"Bring her in here."

On command, Emilio's goons went to the room that I shared with Gia and brought her to Emilio's office. Gia sat in the office chair next to me. She looked at Emilio like she was ready to kill him right there. Her eyes were swollen and red. She looked like she had cried her soul away and there was nothing that I could do to help. Emilio sat down on the other end of his desk and crossed his hands together in front of his face. Emilio let out a long sigh and stared deeply into Gia's eyes. Gia challenged him and stared back.

"You okay?" It wasn't my place to speak out of turn, but I had to know that Gia was alright. She didn't even respond. Gia continued to stare at Emilio as if she had zoned out.

"A better question would be: 'Why did you put our lives at risk by hitting Emilio Sosa in the face?' Or at least, that's what I would be asking."

"You really don't remember me, do you?"

"Remember you? I know you?"

"It's amazing how in a few years you could forget me. Forget what I look like. Forget how many of your facial features that I possess." Gia's words hit me like a ton of bricks. I prayed that she wasn't saying what I thought she was.

"Excuse me?" Emilio was even more confused now than he was originally. I had only known him to have children with his wife, Celeste. With Gia's looming accusation, Emilio would possibly have some explaining to do.

Right when I thought that things couldn't get any worse, Celeste walked in. As soon as she saw Emilio's bruised and somewhat bloody face, she began to ask questions. Emilio didn't hesitate to explain that Gia punched him, and that we were getting to the root of the problem. That was the relationship that I wanted with Gia. Full of honesty. Celeste looked at Gia and her eyes got wide. Gia's face gave off a renewed sense of anger. When she tried to hop over the table to get to Celeste, I had no choice but to grab and hold onto her.

"YOU KEPT MY FATHER AWAY FROM ME!!!" Gia kept repeating the same phrase over and over. A single tear fell from Celeste's left eye.

"I didn't, Giavoni. Your mother kept us away." Celeste's revelation caused Emilio to stare at Gia long and hard.

"Giavoni? Giavoni Sinclaire Sosa…?" Emilio was holding back tears. Gia was no longer trying to fight me to let her go.

"My last name is Allen." The disappointment and regret on Emilio's face was enough to cause Gia to loosen up.

"Your last name was Sosa. Your mother must've changed it."

"Why would she keep me away?"

"She told us that it was in your best interest. She had been left to raise you unprotected. Emilio wasn't always there to protect you. Being his daughter, you would always have a target on your back." Celeste interjected. Gia stared down at the ground. She was defeated. Her mother had kept her away from the only man the she ever knew. She ended up running away from love after that.

It was hard for me to get close to Gia without feeling like there were no strings attached. Gia never experienced the lasting love of any man that crossed her path. All of her flaws and imperfection made me want to love her even harder.

Levi

Lyrik surprised me when she said that she couldn't accept my proposal. I was hoping for a lifetime; now, I just hoped that she could forgive me.

I stayed with Lyrik until they discharged her. I took one step forward and got knocked one step back. Lyrik hadn't said that we were over officially but I felt like it was over. Our relationship was over before it had even begun. Between trying to keep Jazmine away from Lyrik and trying to keep Tyrek's ass out the picture, I was mentally exhausted. I went through so much to prove my love and it still wasn't enough.

I prayed for Lyrik's wellbeing on a daily basis and now that she was pregnant, I felt the need to pray even harder. I wanted Lyrik to understand that I wasn't going to hurt her like the others. My intentions are solely based on her happiness. Until then, we would not be able to thrive. Until Lyrik could understand the strength of my love, I did not see how we would be able to co-exist. Our souls were intertwined. We were already as one. I just wished that she could see it.

Chapter 9
Lyrik

8 weeks pregnant.

The thought of being pregnant would never cease to amaze me. When I was discharged from the hospital, Levi immediately started ordering things for the baby. We didn't even know the gender of the baby yet. Every day there was something new. We visited Claire in the hospital daily. Her car wreck put her in a coma that they weren't even sure that she would awake from. I talked to her all the time. Claire's parents were right by her side and made sure that she was given the best care possible. *How could such a joyous moment in my life be the worst for her?*

Levi wasted no time preparing my original room for the baby as a nursery. Sahara and

Jamal even came to help when they weren't visiting Claire at the hospital. My sister and I were finally getting along and acting how sisters should.

I wasn't complete, however. I wanted to see Levi smile again. He only smiled whenever we discussed the baby.

The constant act of ignoring each other and him accepting that I needed space just proved to me how much I didn't deserve him. Levi was supportive, caring and he was all around the perfect man. I couldn't do anything other than love him. Through the pain and tears, Levi was there to comfort me. He made it known that I was his woman and I didn't have to worry about anything. Whatever I wanted, Levi worked hard to provide it. *Stop being a dumbass and accept his proposal.*

Levi was so patient and loving. The thought of losing Levi because of my pigheaded, stubbornness was enough to make me see that just because I wasn't ready to talk to my mom, didn't mean that we shouldn't have the conversation.

I knew that Levi wasn't going to even attempt to help me after what happened last time; so, I wanted until he got in the shower before I texted my mother and scheduled a meet as if I was Levi. I needed answers that only she could provide. I needed the healing.

***

When I arrived at the Hampton Inn, I was nervous. I was about to face my mother and it was every bit possible that I wouldn't be able to contain myself. *Room 123, room 123, room 123... Room 123.* As I stood in front of my mom's hotel door, I couldn't help but hesitate on whether or not I should knock on the door. I was 8 weeks pregnant and vulnerable. I took a deep breath to shake off my nerves then knocked on the door.

"Who is it?" I couldn't bring myself to say anything. "Who is it?" More silence. When she opened the door, the marks of my attack were evident but fading. We stared at each other for a moment. Without warning, she grabbed me and hugged me. She hugged me and I flinched. It was my natural reaction to her touching me. I never experienced a hug from my mother. The norm was me running into my room and locking the door whenever she came home drunk; I'd hope and pray that she didn't break into my room for a routine beating.

"Please stop." She let me go but I couldn't look at her. I stared at my feet.

"What's wrong?" *Did she really just ask me what was wrong?*

"Do you not remember what my childhood was like? You didn't hug me. You abused me in damn near every way possible. The only crime you didn't commit was sexual abuse. You were my first bully. You beat me damn near to death. You told me that I wasn't good enough. That I wasn't going to be anything. I had to skip my high school graduation because my face and body were covered in bruises. You constantly picked on me and because you were my mother, I didn't say anything. I suffered in silence until I couldn't suffer anymore. I wanted to end my life and I contemplated that decision often. You admitted that you hated me on more than one occasion. But then you get clean and show up to my house a few years later and you think that just because you said that you were sorry, I shouldn't hold any grudges? That everything should just be okay?" I hadn't even noticed my voice was cracking and I was crying. My tears burned as they rolled down my face. These weren't tears of sadness, these were tears of anger. I was done with my mother feeling entitled to being in my life just because she birthed me. The way that she treated me, she should've just aborted me.

"I'm sorry, Lyrik. I don't know what else to say. I don't know what else to do. I was wrong. I shouldn't have treated you that way. I'm so sorry."

"Your sorrys mean nothing to me. Don't contact me or Levi again." I turned to walk away but I stopped myself. "I forgive you but make no mistake; you are not going to be a part of my life. I've washed my hands of you." I was tired of carrying around the pain that I had to endure through the years. I had to forgive her for all of her wrongdoing but not for her. For me. I wasn't going to continue to be a victim. I wasn't a victim. I was a survivor. A warrior. I endured shit that most people never have to; especially not from a damn parent that was supposed to protect them.

***

I wasn't in the mood for Levi's constant pestering. 'Is the baby okay? Do you need anything? Are you hungry?' As cute as it was, I just didn't feel like hearing it after seeing my mother. Levi could sense that I was tense. *He could always sense my emotions.*

"You okay? You not talking much. Did I do something?" I instantly felt bad for giving him the cold shoulder for over a month. Anytime I was in a bad mood, he instantly thought that my bad mood came from something that he did.

"What? Levi, no. I just – it's nothing." I wasn't sure if I should tell Levi about the visit that I had with my mother or not. Keeping it a secret was killing me and I didn't need this kind of stress.

"Okay. Well, do you want to help me plan a gender reveal? The baby shower?"

"Levi, I'm only 8 weeks. I don't find out the gender until later on."

"Okay, but there's nothing wrong with looking at some ideas. Planning ahead saves time." Levi shrugged as he brought over his computer for me to look at baby shower and gender reveal ideas on the internet. *What did I do to deserve such a man?*

I couldn't even focus on the ideas that Levi was presenting to me. I had fucked up our relationship because I wasn't able to face my mother. I made him the enemy when he just wanted to be an ally.

"Levi, did you really want to marry me? Not just because I'm pregnant but you wanted to actually marry me?" Levi's position on the couch straightened up.

"Of course. Lyrik, I wanted to marry you before I found out that you were pregnant. It just never seemed like the right time to ask. I love you." Levi kissed my lips and I knew that he was telling the truth. *He wants to spend the rest of his life with me.*

"Then ask me again."

"What?"

"Ask me again, Levi." A sly smile came across Levi's face and I knew that I made his day. He got off the couch and ran to the back. I could hear Levi accidentally breaking shit in the distance. *What in the hell?* When he came back into the den, he had the black velvet box that he originally gave me when he asked. I rolled my eyes and gave a soft chuckle. Levi got on one knee in front of me and took my left hand in his.

"Lyrik, I've loved you since we were kids. That love eventually grew over time and I'm glad that we get to experience that love through our first child together. I couldn't imagine a life without you. So, with this ring I ask you – No. I beg you to be mine. Lyrik Mareecia Moore, will you do me the honor of becoming my wife – my soulmate for life?"

"Yes." With tears in both of our eyes, Levi slid the ring onto my finger, and we kissed. My life wasn't always a happy but at least I got to have my happy ending.

Gia

My father wasted no time trying to make up for lost time. I wasn't excited about the idea, but I learned the hard way that sometimes it's just best to accept free gifts. His connections meant a lot to Duke; I wasn't going to jeopardize that.

This man openly admitted to abandoning me just because my mother told him to. There was nothing that him or his ditzy ass wife could do to change how I felt. I was over everybody thinking that they could just leave me high and dry then waltz back into my life like nothing happened.

"Gia? Gia? You good?" I haven't been paying attention to Duke calling my name. We were getting groceries from the mainland and Emilio made sure that I was well protected.

"I'm fine. Just spaced out." I gave Duke a fake smile and he smiled back. I didn't like lying to him but as Emilio's first born – legitimate or not – I had full rights to claiming his empire after his death. I had no intentions of leaving this place until after I got what was rightfully mine.

"You think that this is ripe enough?" Duke asked. He held a cantaloupe up to my face playfully and I pushed his arm. Duke was always doing things to distract me. Things he knew would make me smile. That would be a problem. Distractions were not going to be good for what I had planned. Duke was not going to be good for what I had planned.

Duke

Gia had been out of it since we arrived on the island. She didn't speak much. Emilio showered her with gifts and apologized to her daily for not being in her life. The thought of him being her father made sense. She didn't understand how to love or be loved because he wasn't present in her life. Gia was a lost soul. Emilio was like a father figure to me; I knew that I had to ask him for permission to marry his daughter if I did nothing else.

When Gia and I left the market, Emilio was waiting for us at the pier with a yacht. He hugged Gia and I could see the joy beaming from his face. His first born, his first love; he was so upset about missing most of her life.

"Let's go. Celeste is cooking. And trust me, you don't want to be late for dinner." Emilio was the happiest that I had seen him in years. Gia sparked something in him like she does for me.

"Good cause I'm hungry as hell."

"You always hungry." Gia rolled her eyes and laughed. She was like a different person now. Emilio joined in on the laughter and I figured that this would be the best time to talk to Emilio about Gia. I nodded to Emilio to let him know that we needed to talk.

"We'll be right back." I kissed Gia on the forehead then proceeded to follow Emilio to one of the guest rooms so that we could talk. I felt nervous and I never got nervous when talking to Emilio. We talked about everything but talking about Gia felt forbidden.

"What's on your mind, Duke?" Emilio was all business. He was looking me in the eye and could sense the anxiety running throughout my body.

"It's about Gia."

"What about her?" Emilio's defensive stance made me start sweating bullets. *Hell, if I say the wrong thing, I just might catch one.*

"I just wanted to ask you for permission for – I mean I really want to marry Gia. We haven't known each other long but she's definitely earned a place in my heart. I just –" Emilio place his hand up to stop me from speaking. The grim look on his face suggested that there was no way in hell I'd ever marry Gia. Let alone look at her again after my request.

"So, you want to marry my daughter? Why?"

"Sir?" I was genuinely confused by the question. Gia meant the world to me.

"Why do you want to marry my daughter? As a trophy? She's pretty, right?"

"Gia is a beautiful woman but he beauty on the inside is what I'm attracted to. She's round around the edges but that's what makes her special. She has the cutest face she makes when she's mad. She's a hustler and she doesn't accept anything less than the best. She will chew your ass out but love you all the same. I just want to be the best man that I can be for her. I'm asking your permission now because I found out that you were her father. I've already asked, and I plan on showing her what her life will be like with me as her husband. Asking you was just a kindness. A formality that I decided to extend." Emilio looked me up and down. The stiffness in his face changed into a smile.

"You got balls. Don't know why I'm surprised. You didn't get this far by keeping your mouth closed. That outspokenness is what set you apart from the rest. I would be honored to bestow my blessing upon the union. I already consider you my son. Fate clearly brought you together." Emilio extended his hand towards me and I shook his hand. We hugged it out and for the first time in a while, I felt conflicted. I said that I would do anything for Gia, but I had never even thought of killing Emilio until now. His abandonment took a toll on her. I could see that she was hiding the pain behind her eyes. It was my job to get rid of that pain.

***

When we got back to the island, Gia's sister welcomed us at the pier. Lily was so excited to see her big sister until she hopped aboard and hugged Gia tight. Caralina and Catalina were spitting images of Gia. Daisy and Lily looked like Celeste. Daisy walked up to the yacht and stood next to her sisters.

"Mom said hurry up cause the food is done!" She yelled to Emilio. She laughed and Gia picked up Lily and carried her all the way to the house. Gia and Lily acted more like mother and daughter than sisters. Lily wanted to be around Gia 24/7 and Gia welcomed her presence. Her sisters made her happy. This was a problem. Gia hated Emilio and Celeste, but she didn't share that same disdain with her sisters. Everything that I had planned wasn't going to work out the way that was beneficial to everyone involved in the scenario but Gia's happiness is all I cared about.

Levi

Lyrik and I decided on a courthouse wedding so that we could enjoy planning the gender reveal and baby shower. Lyrik was getting up there in size; so, she refused to walk down anyone's aisle pregnant. I didn't blame her. As I looked into her eyes, I could see that the love that we had for each other was eternal. I looked around the courthouse at all these strangers that were about to witness us getting married. My stomach was in knots but I knew what I wanted.

"Do you take Lyrik to be your lawfully wedded wife?" I took a deep breath to keep the tears from falling.

"I do."

"Lyrik, do you take Levi to be your lawfully wedded husband?" She flashed me a smile. The most beautiful smile that I've ever seen.

"I do."

"I know pronounce you man and wife. You may kiss your bride."

I lunged at Lyrik with the most passionate kiss that I could muster. She was my everything and now she was my wife. The others in the courthouse clapped in celebration of our union. Lyrik was officially Mrs. Hendrix and there was nothing that could make this moment any better.

Lyrik sudden doubled over in pant. The khaki pants that she had on started to fill with blood and she started to panic. She screamed in pain and I immediately knew what was happening.

"SOMEBODY CALL AN AMBULANCE!"

Chapter 10
Lyrik

"I'm sorry…" The worst words that I've ever had to hear. The words that the doctor told me when it was confirmed that I had a miscarriage. I felt like my entire world was ending. I may have not wanted to be pregnant originally, but I got ready for the sake of my child. *10 weeks pregnant.*

I couldn't believe that the happiest day of my life was also the worst. Through it all, Levi never left my side. From the hospital ride to finding out about the miscarriage. Levi stayed by my side. I cried in his arms and he let me know that it was okay to cry. I didn't have to keep it in. I didn't have to keep calm or pretend that I wasn't hurting. *I am hurting.* The life that I carried inside of me no longer existed. I cried. That's all I knew to do. I was hurt. I was angry. I cursed God every chance I got because he caused my pain. He was selfish with the precious gift that he bestowed upon me. Levi always claimed that 'things happened for a reason', but what was the reason for this?

I was a childless mother. No one would be able to understand that pain. The pain of seeing those lines on the pregnancy test, picking out names, guessing about whether it would be a boy or a girl… only to have that fantasy snatched from you. Who could understand that? Who could understand the idea of your body rejecting the child that you wanted? *No one could understand… Could they?*

After being discharged, Levi and I didn't talk about the baby. It was too surreal. He brought me home, gave me a bath, then tucked me in. I was like a mindless zombie. I didn't want to do anything other than cry. I cried and cried and cried and cried… Still no baby. My child was gone, and no amount of tears were going to bring him or her back. *Why me?*

I cried and repeated the same question over and over again. *Why me? Why me?* Was God even listening? I asked the same question over and over, but he didn't give me a response. I was forced to endure this pain. Levi knew that I was hurt but he couldn't possibly imagine the pain. The physical, emotional, and psychological pain of having to deal with the loss of a child. In a few weeks, he would be fine, and he would want to try again. Me? I would be in pain for the rest of my life. I tried to figure out why this happened. I tried to see that light at the end of the tunnel. Nothing. This was a pain that I had never felt before. I got nicked with a bullet, beaten senseless and damn near to death by my own mother, and I still didn't know a pain even remotely close to this. I just wanted to roll over and die.

***

Then next day after I was discharged from the hospital, I didn't even go to class. I couldn't. I didn't want to deal with the constant questions about the baby. 'What happened? Are you okay? I'm praying for you.' I didn't need prayer and I damn sure wasn't asking for it. Levi hovered over me like a moth to a flame and it was the most annoying thing ever. As annoying as it was though, I appreciated it. It just let me know that he cared.

The reality of the situation, however, was that I wanted to be alone. I decided that since I couldn't do anything else... Why not read? I browsed the bookshelf on the other side of the room, and I could not decide on a book to read. Levi came in the room and saw me looking over the books to figure out which to read.

"Any idea about what you wanna read? I got a few idea's in mind." I rolled my eyes playfully then gave Levi a look.

"Like what?"

"Either *The Missing Piece* or *Falling Up* by Shel Silverstein." Levi continued search for something throughout the room.

"What are you looking for?"

"My phone."

"It's in the bathroom where you left it." I grabbed *Falling Up* off the shelf and decided to sit on the bed to read it. I needed something to get my mind off of my miscarriage so that I can stop crying for at least a few hours. I turned a few pages and eventually got to 'Diving Board'. The poems made me smile and forget my pain for a small while. But the pain of losing my child still made me go crazy. I was still saddened by it. I didn't know what else to do so I took a shower and got ready for bed even though it was midday. Levi didn't bother me. I think that he understood what I was going through. Even though I originally felt that there was no way that he could understand how I felt… I was obviously wrong. The hurt and anger clouded my judgement. I just wished that the pain would cease and that there would be light in my life again.

Gia

The time finally came to go back home. It was the last day of business for Duke and Emilio, and I was ready to go. Pretending to be happy was starting to take a toll on my life. My father made a life with Celeste that he couldn't seem to do with my own mother. I had four other sisters that I never thought I would get along with. They were the only saving grace about the entire trip. I may have hated my father, but my sisters were mine to protect. I was the oldest now. I looked at myself in the mirror. The all white, flowy sundress that Duke had purchased for me was absolutely beautiful.

"Gia, Emilio wants to see you." I was still staring at myself and fixing my hair when one of my father's goons came into my room. Emilio and Duke had been scarce all day. I guess it was my turn for attention.

When I walked out into the garden, everybody in attendance was dressed in white. I looked around and saw my sisters were all giggly. I was confused as the motioned me to walk towards my father and Duke. Celeste was standing off to the side and several armed guards were standing in a circle around us.

"What's going on?"

"Giavoni Sinclaire Sosa-Allen, do you wish to marry Duke?" Emilio caught me by surprise with his question. My eyes got wide instantly.

"I—uh—"

"Do you feel like you can't live without him?"

"Yes."

"You love him?"

"Yes."

"So, why the hesitation?" Emilio had a point. I was falling in love with Duke more and more each day.

"Duke, I will marry you." I looked Duke in his eyes and his eyes started beaming. The excitement in his eyes told me everything that I needed to know.

"Good. I'll defend you, protect you, and love you with all the strength in my body." Duke kissed my lips then snapped his fingers.

Almost instantly the sound of gunshots rang into the air. Everybody ducked to the floor, but it was no use. This was a professional hit and Duke had chosen his targets carefully. Emilio was the first to get hit. Headshots only. I looked around the garden to try and find my sisters. I found Lily laying under the body of a deceased man. I ignored all signs that told me that I shouldn't try to save her for fear of being hit. If I wouldn't have saved her, she would've suffocated to death. Blood was being shed and Duke was the cause. I told myself not to take that chance, to save my own life, but I couldn't just let her die. I made Duke let go of me and I ran as fast as I could to reach Lily. I tried to push the body off of her. She had two gunshot wounds to the stomach. The blood was pumping out faster than I could do anything. Catalina was hiding in the nearby bushes when one of Duke's men grabbed her by her hair and dragged her to where they could all see her. Daisy tried to stab him in the shoulder with a small pocket knife. He laughed then gave her a powerful backhand that made her unconscious.

"Hey! Find her other sister!" I put pressure on Lily's wound, but nothing stopped the massive amounts of blood that came out of her wounds. Within minutes, Lily let go of her last breath. I began to wail. Duke had got what he wanted at the cost of my youngest sister's life. Duke touched my shoulder. He caressed my shoulder to let me know that he was sorry for my loss. I got up and continuously bang on his chest. The Lily's blood stained his white V-neck. Almost my entire family was slaughtered in an instant and I didn't know how to feel. I wanted Emilio dead, but I didn't want this. My plan was more calculating. I was upset with Duke for killing my target faster and with more precision than I could. The only thing that I truly felt upset by was Lily's murder. I just hoped that Caralina was able to get away and never turned back.

My hopes and dreams were crushed yet again when another one of Duke's goon brought Caralina back. She looked like she had put up a fight.

"Now what? You're going to kill my sisters?" Duke looked at me then down at Lily's lifeless body.

"No. I had no intention of you, or your sisters, being hurt. I loved Lily, and I'll do whatever it takes to make that right by all of you. I saw the hurt in your eyes. Every time you looked at Emilio, you saw him leaving you and your mother with nothing. Isn't this what you wanted?" I looked at Duke tearfully. Caralina and Catalina saw Lily's lifeless body and wailed. Daisy was starting to come to when she heard all the commotion. I walked away from Duke to mourn with my sisters. They had to know that I didn't plan any of this. We mourned Lily together.

Out of the blue, another gunshot went off and I heard Duke groan in the distance. Emilio had mustered up enough strength to shoot Duke in his side. Duke fell to his knees and curled up on the ground in pain. I started to rush to his side until I saw Lily's body right next to him. I just sat there and let him cry out in pain. Begging me for assistance. My love for him and my love for my sister's had me torn in two. His goons were at his side and barking orders for me and my sisters to go into the house. We did as we were told; and not long after, a doctor was walking into the garden area to save Duke's life. He saw the massacre before him and stopped dead in his tracks. I rushed my sisters to my room where I had them bathe and change clothes immediately. I wasn't about to let Duke ruin our lives. I knew him. He was going to pull through. Duke wasn't the one that I was terrified of. I was scared of what his goons would do to four women when Duke wasn't around or able to do anything. I wasn't about to let my sisters be subjected to that.

I had to deal with shit like that my entire life. I wasn't about to let his goon take advantage of me or my sisters. If I had to choose, I would sacrifice myself for them any day of the week.

***

I was already packed so it didn't take long for me to get some clothes for my sisters and make a run for it. We left through the door in my room that lead to the balcony. We were parallel to the ground; so, all we had to do was get past Duke's guards. With the rocks all around, I picked up the smallest ones that I could find.

"What are you doing?" Catalina asked.

"You'll see. Get back."

I hurled a rock at the nearest guard and ducked. When he turned around, he saw another guard was just coming back from his bathroom break and instantly assumed the worst. They started arguing and ended up fist fighting. I took my sisters with me and we ran for the pier. I decided that the yacht would slow us down; so, we took a smaller boat. I got my sisters safely on the boat before I got aboard myself. The sound of us starting the engine, caused an uproar. By the time Duke's goons got to the pier, we were almost to the mainland. I never knew that I would be torn between the love of my life and family, but Duke made it clear that we were both full of shit. We constantly kept secrets from each other. He came up with this scheme but expected me to believe that Lily's death was an accident. He knew that with my sisters being in the crowd, it was a possibility of any of them getting hit.

Duke didn't give a shit about my sisters. As long as he had me, that's all he cared about. The fucked-up part is…I understood. I loved him the same way. I would air out his entire family, if it meant that he would be mine and only mine. That kind of love wasn't really love. It was an obsession. I was toxic. I saw what that kind of love did to LaBrielle and I wasn't about to deal with that myself. I refused to love any man to death.

Levi

I went to Grandma Patty's house because she said that she had to speak to me. Lyrik just got to the point where she would eat something, and I didn't want to leave her alone for a long period of time.

I got out of the car and ran up the stairs to her front door. I rang the doorbell and didn't get an answer. I knocked on the door and the door opened slightly. I cautiously waked in the house to see Tyrek sitting on the couch watching tv.

"So, you didn't hear the bell ringing?"

"Nope." This nonchalant act that Tyrek had going on was pissing me off. His presence was draining.

"Yeah. Whatever. Where Grandma?"

"She left. She'll be back." Tyrek turned off the tv and got off the couch and strolled towards me. "What I wanna know is: why are you here?"

"She asked me to come over. Now, back the fuck up before I beat yo ass again."

"Yeah aight. I don't want no problems, killa. Just know that Lyrik mine. Stay away from her."

"She's yours? She lives with me and we're married. *You* stay away from her." I turned to leave when Tyrek put a plastic bag over my head. I elbowed him hard enough for him to lose his grip and I took off the bag and headed for the door. Tyrek tripped me with his leg and closed the door. I tried to fight him off and even got a few licks in.

"Where you going, baby bro?"

He placed the bag back over my head and I clawed at the bag. My vision started to get blurry and I hoped that I lived to see another day.

Lyrik

Levi had been gone for an hour and it wasn't like him to not even shoot me a text. I decided to go to the hospital after he left so that I could visit Claire. She was still unresponsive, but she was breathing on her own. She looked like a little porcelain doll.

"I lost the baby. I got married to Levi. I just wish you were here. Here for me to talk to. Miguel visits regularly. Did you know that? He still loves you." I sniffled as tears began to fall. I grabbed a tissue from by the sink in the hospital room and wiped my eyes. I kissed Claire on the forehead then made my way to Grandma Patty's. It was going on two hours and Levi hadn't said anything. I called and didn't get an answer. When I pulled up, Levi's car was sitting in front on her gate. Levi was definitely here. Levi never gave me an explanation for why Grandma Patty wanted to see him, but it had to be important. Grandma Patty didn't ask anyone to come and visit.

I knocked on the door and didn't get an answer. I knocked again. Still no answer. My intuition told me that the door was unlocked. I grabbed the handle and opened the door. Something didn't seem right.

I ran up the stairs and knocked on Grandma Patty's bedroom door. When her door opened slightly, I pushed it open the rest of the way and saw Grandma Patty in her bed with her throat slit. Blood was everywhere and Levi was nowhere in sight. I gasped at the sight of her like that. I started to tear up, but I couldn't get distracted. I closed the door back and ran to the kitchen. If someone was still here, then I need to protect myself. I grabbed the biggest knife that I could find.

"AHHH!!!" I heard screaming and instantly thought of Levi. *He's in trouble.*

The screams sounded like they were coming from the basement. I carefully crept down the basement stairs and hid behind some boxes that Grandma Patty had lined up. Tyrek had Levi bound to a chair and was beating his ass and burning him with a cigarette.

"Ain't too tough now, are you? Got a few tools here. Let's see if we can take a few of those teeth out." Tyrek reached for the pliers and I knew that this was the only chance I had to save Levi. Tyrek went to pull out one of Levi's teeth in the back when I stabbed him. I stabbed him repeatedly in the back until he fell to the floor. I checked his pulse and noticed that he was still breathing. I untied Levi and dragged him back upstairs and out the door. We called the police and they were there in a matter of minutes. I told them about how I found Grandma Patty and how Tyrek had Levi tied up. They gave me enough time to talk to Levi myself.

"Did you find out what Grandma Patty wanted?"

"No. I think he made her call me before he killed her." Levi's answer made me want to cry. Grandma Patty did right by everyone. Everybody loved her.

"Why would he do something like that?"

"I asked her to help me find my real mother." I gave Levi a confused look.

"But what does that have to do with Tyrek? And why did I not know that you were adopted?"

"Tyrek and Tone were my birth brothers. I found out in high school. That's one of the real reasons that I left." Levi avoided my gaze.

"Why—"

"Sorry to interrupt but there's no one in the basement." The police officer interrupted. He let us know that they had Tyrek's blood samples from the knife but he was no longer in the basement. The EMTs brought out Grandma Patty's body on a stretcher and my body went limp. If it wasn't one thing, it was another. It was like death surrounded us at every possible turn. I was worried for myself and Levi. With Tyrek on the move, I could only imagine what would happen. Tyrek made it clear that he wasn't going to let go of me and his obsession only grew with each day. The fact that Levi was his brother and Levi had the better life just drove him even more crazy. Everything actually made sense now. The back and forth with him and Tone. The jealousy. Tone trying to talk to me, being spiteful. I was always just a ploy to get back at Tyrek. I was sick of this shit. I just wanted everything to be over. I just wanted to believe in my happily ever after again.

Levi

The ambulance brought me to the ER to make sure that I was okay and that Tyrek didn't do too much damage. I was just ready to go home. I knew that Lyrik had questions about my real parents and why I kept everything a secret. I didn't even know how to respond when I found out. It was a mixture of emotions and I know that it was the same for her.

"You okay?" Lyrik was standing right in front of me as we waited for the doctor to come back. I could tell that she was concerned but I didn't want to talk about it. Tyrek had gotten the best of me and if it weren't for Lyrik showing up when she did, I would have been mangled. I was the provider, the protector. But I couldn't even protect myself. I let my guard down and almost died because of it.

"I'm fine."

"So, we're just not gonna ever talk about what happened?"

"I would prefer not to."

"Levi, you kept the biggest secret of all time from me. Why?" Lyrik was extremely concerned but pissed off at the same time.

"How do you think I felt? I ain't wanna deal with that. I already hated Tyrek but the thought of him being my brother too? I was okay with Tone being my brother. Tone was cool. Tyrek was the asshole that everybody hated."

"Tyrek wasn't this bad. I don't know what happened."

"He lost you. When you left, he probably realized that he wanted you back. I came into the picture and everything went into high gear. He knew that I hated him, and he hated me."

"So, that makes it okay?"

"No. That makes him jealous." My response clearly struck a nerve because Lyrik went to sit in a nearby chair. She put her face in her hands and let out a long sigh. I felt the same way and I knew that Tyrek wasn't going to be gone for good. He was already hiding from the feds. Nothing was going to stop Tyrek but death.

Epilogue
Tyrek

Lyrik did whatever to get under my skin. There was no way in hell that she loved that pretty boy ass nigga more than she loved me. The strength of her love is the only thing that kept me going. Lyrik was the love of my life and I wasn't about to let her go so easily.

"Yes. He's in the basement. Please hurry." Lyrik's voice was like a siren song. I couldn't stay long. The police would be here soon, and I needed medical attention. I ran out the back door and went to the south side. It was only one person who I could trust at this point.

"Ya lil girlfriend fucked you up. Lil bitch got heart."

"Don't call her out of her name. She's a better woman that you could ever be."

"Then why you here with me and not with her?" I couldn't bring myself to even reply. The pain in my back was numbed by the sting of the sewing needle that was stitching my back together.

"I thought so. You're a mama's boy. Always was."

"I was. Until you traded me for crack. You let that man do whatever he wanted to me." My sadistic mother chuckled at the thought of my pain. She didn't care about anyone but herself.

"You act like he killed you. You survived that. I killed him for what he did to you. You don't have to keep bringing it up. Besides…

You were always my strongest, and favorite child. That's why it was so hard for me to give you up." She kissed the top of my head then continued to stitch up my back. My mama would always say that I was her favorite of all her children. Levi and Tone were disposable to her. I never understood how that could be true when she traded me for a couple of crack rocks. I was a child. I was only ten years old when she allowed him the sodomize me. I screamed for help, but she was too high to do anything or care. When she finally woke up, I was bleeding. She took me to the hospital and left me there. When she came back, she told me that she took care of him. Since then, my innocence was gone. I never allowed anyone to get too close to me. I proved my masculinity through the various females I smashed left and right. I couldn't allow anyone to know what happened to me.

I was going to keep my pain to myself. Fuck anybody who had an issue.

Claire

"Her vitals are normal. Only thing left is to hope that she wakes up." I could hear the nurse speaking and I tried to open my eyes. It felt like it had been months since I had the wreck. I would try to open my eyes to no avail. Today was different. I tried to open my eyes and my eyes finally began to flutter. I saw Miguel and my parents with the nurse at the other end of my bed. I knew that trying to talk may have been pushing it, but they had to see that I was okay.

I tried to talk but only weird sounds came out. *Fuck! I forgot about this tube down my throat.* I continued making noises until Miguel looked my way.

"She's awake!" Everybody rushed to my side and the nurse took the feeding tube out of my throat. I looked around the room. My parents looked so stressed. Me being in the hospital had to have taken a toll on them. I looked at Miguel. Lyrik was right. He did still love me. The look on his face said so. He was right here by my side. I shed a tear and Miguel kissed my forehead. I was so glad to be awake.

www.ingramcontent.com/pod-product-compliance
Lightning Source LLC
LaVergne TN
LVHW091634070526
838199LV00044B/1066